A MEN OF SIEGE NOVELLA

LACHLAN

BEX DANE

All my love,
Bex Dane

Published by Larken Romance

First edition January 2019

Cover by Elizabeth Mackey Designs

Become a VIP reader

Sign up to Bex Dane's VIP reader team and receive exclusive bonus content including;

- Free books

- Behind-the-scenes secrets no one else knows

- Deleted scenes

- Advanced Reader Copies and first look at cover reveals

Visit bexdane.com

Chapter 1

―――

L achlan

Not Nevada.

Not Nevada.

Not Nevada.

None of the women in this filthy strip club looked anything like her.

The red pen in my head crossed off "stripping for a dealer" from the list of worst possible outcomes for Nevada.

A much longer list remained. A list that haunted my every thought.

Nevada tortured.

Nevada raped.

Nevada dead.

Eight months I'd been looking for her. My best friend's little sister had turned into a ghost. Found her dog at her friend's apartment. She canceled her utilities and paid a year's rent ahead of time. Her boss at the Port Authority said she'd quit four years ago.

Nevada lied to me. Why? Whatever it was, she should've trusted me with it. Or I should've been the man she needed me to be so she could confide in me.

My fist balled and pounded against the wall. As if I could push these thoughts through my hand, into the wall, and have them evaporate into the Boston night.

Stay on task, Cutlass. Focus on the op and close the deal. Forget about Nevada for a goddamn second.

A waitress in a tight, black outfit walked by, all tits and ass. She made eye contact and an inviting smile stretched across her face. She kept her eyes on me as she passed, dipping her chin and flashing her lashes. If I wanted to, I could take her to the back, get high with her, and fuck away all this frustration. Tempting. A temporary relief from reality. But no. Not me. I'd never surrender to the lure of a quick high and a meaningless fuck.

Not again.

Johnny Blanco came strutting toward me, trying to look cool by walking with a limp. His dirty-blond hair stuck up like he'd worked too hard to make a casual mess. He wasn't any more Italian than me, but the Dubare Syndicate didn't discriminate too much when it came to soldiers to sell narcotics for the Italian Mafia. They needed feet on the ground and took in anyone they thought they could control. Johnny stayed smart, wearing sharp suits, lots of bling. He'd avoided getting hooked on heroin, but he had no problem making a profit off the poor souls who weren't as fortunate.

In seven weeks, I'd bought two kilos of heroin from Johnny and earned enough trust to set up this meet with his supplier, Darin Aquino.

Johnny stopped in front of me, scanning my shoulders for signs of a holster and my waist for a gun imprint. He wouldn't find one. I came "unarmed" per his instructions, but I still had a knife at my ankle, a wire in my watch, and an FBI tag team waiting in a van in the alley.

"This way, Capioni."

All I had to do was make the deal with Aquino and give the signal—*It's been a pleasure doing business with you.*

Blanco's shoulder twitched, and the scent of fear came off him, but not enough for me to act. It would take a lot more than a little sweat on Blanco's forehead to force me to give up on Aquino.

I followed him through a narrow corridor to an apartment at the back of the club. He knocked twice and entered a room cemented in the eighties. Green and brown shag carpet, a hanging lamp with blue balls as bulbs, wooden curtain rods with big pointy finials. The ancient tweed couches looked like they'd seen plenty of action. If we needed DNA, the forensics team would hit those first. The only other person in the room, besides Aquino, was a girl bending forward into one of those old avocado fridges.

"Darin, this is Lake Capioni." Johnny introduced me to Darin Aquino, an aging dealer from the South End, and the owner of this club. His glossy eyes appraised me, his hands folded over his distended belly.

"Sit down, have a seat." He motioned to a rattan chair across the table from him.

I took the seat and checked out the girl again.

Her denim miniskirt, tattered at the bottom, rode up in the back. I caught a hint of bare ass cheek. Her gray sweatshirt hung off her shoulders. She was skinnier than Nevada, with darker hair, but about the same height. I hadn't seen her face, but my spidey senses told me she didn't belong here. If this went south, I'd have to make sure to keep her out of the crossfire.

Johnny took a seat to my right. "Babe, bring me a beer."

"Okay, Johnny," the girl answered from the kitchen. Again, my intuition screamed something wasn't right with her.

Everything else appeared legit. A textbook reversal. I'd get this bust done, finish the paperwork, and return to searching for Nevada. The girl was the wildcard though.

She closed the fridge and walked to Johnny with two beers dangling between her fingers.

And holy shit.

Fuck me.

What in the goddamn hell?

The universe stopped spinning.

My gaze locked on forest-green eyes so deep I'd lost myself in them many times.

Tawny freckles peppered her nose.

I tore my gaze from hers to check the rest of her. Skinnier than I liked to see her, but still petite and curvy.

Her signature red mane changed to a muddy brown, pressed flat to her head and hanging over her shoulders like dead weight instead of flying wild.

Sweet mother of god.

Nevada Lacy was very much alive.

After searching all of New England, I found her in a strip club during a drug bust.

Her shoulders rocked back, her foot slipping out to the side.

My mouth dropped open, wanting to say something—anything—to her. Our first words in more than half a year.

My Nev. *I found you.*

Her gaze narrowed on my three-week-old beard. Did she recognize me? Her eyes tipped back up to mine. There. I saw it. A flash of recognition, her pupils widening ever so slightly. Her lips twitched. Nothing else gave her away except those two infinitesimal blips.

I expected a stronger reaction to seeing me. She had to feel the volatile energy coming off me.

My hands gripped the arms of the chair, ready to pounce on her the second she blew my cover.

But she didn't.

Instead, she shrugged and turned away, her face tired and bored.

What the hell was that?

Either she was pretending or she'd forgotten me and all we had before.

While my heart raced in my chest, she handed Johnny an open beer and then proceeded to sit her ass down on Johnny's lap.

My Nev sat her ass on a fucking drug dealer's lap.

Without my years of training, I'd lose my shit.

What the fuck are you doing here sitting on Johnny Blanco's lap?

She leaned back against his chest. He wrapped a possessive hand around her bare thigh.

My blood boiled. If I had my firearm, I'd shoot his hand off her leg.

Searching her appearance for clues, some hint this was a farce, I found nothing. Dark circles ringed her eyes. Strands of her normally vibrant red hair were dark and frayed. She turned her head toward Aquino like a spaced-out junkie waiting for her next high.

"That's Nev." He used the shortened version of her real name. That meant she wasn't pretending. Nevada had really become a junkie. "She's Johnny's girl." Darin's voice sounded suspicious. I need to rein it in, or I'd blow this op.

One deep breath and I was good.

Nevada was a junkie. Fine. I could help her detox. Get her clean. Bring her back to me and her family. At least she wasn't dead or kidnapped.

What grated on me the most was finding her deep inside Dubare territory. In the heart of Luigi Greco's circle of influence. The man murdered her parents in cold blood, and she sat here with one of his dealers as if she wasn't betraying their memory and everything her family stood for, died for...

"Well ain't you pretty... Nev." I made my Boston accent thick, like it used to be before the Navy trained it out of me. Thick in a way she had to recognize my voice saying her name.

Her eyes popped open and she started to fidget, pulling in her skirt, tugging her shirt closer to her neck. She sat up straight in Johnny's lap.

Johnny scowled at me. "You bring the cash?"

I pulled the envelope with twenty grand in hundreds from my jacket pocket.

Nevada's lame-ass boyfriend was not only a dealer but dumb enough to get involved in trafficking across state lines. Time to put Johnny and Darin out of business. Not sure where that would leave Nevada, but I had a job to do. "You bring the H?"

Nevada stood up and paced to the window, scratching her arms.

I tensed as Darin reached into a backpack by his feet. He pulled out a block of heroin and a supply bag. "You test my stash first." He untied and unrolled the rig containing hypodermic needles, a spoon, a lighter, and a razor blade. He cut into the brick, and we all watched as he prepared three syringes.

"Nev and I only use our own stash," Johnny spoke quickly.

"Your stash is my stash. What's the difference?" Aquino raised an eyebrow at Johnny's protest.

"We prepare our own H, Darin. Why you need me to take yours?"

Something was wrong here.

"You shoot up this needle right now or you're a cop. You too, Lake. Shoot it up, test the purity. If you don't, you're a cop."

"I ain't no cop." *I am a spook though.* "I'm happy to take a ride." Expecting this, the FBI had applied a prosthetic piece of skin to my elbow.

Johnny, real stupid, continued to take a stand. "Just me, not Nev. I'll take it, not her. She's not in good shape right now."

"Both of you or no deal. You don't get your cut and we all leave." Darin sat back in his chair and leveled his eyes on Johnny.

Nevada came back to the table. "It's okay, Johnny. I want it. I know it's clean. I need it." She held out her arm, showing off the bruises and track marks there. She gave me a belligerent look like she wanted to prove something to me. But her arm was shaking.

"You don't have to." Johnny gave her one last out.

Take it, Nev. Take the out.

"I'm ready."

Fuck.

Darin grinned as he handed—first to me, then Johnny, then Nev—a loaded syringe. The tube around my bicep snapped into place, and I shot the heroin into my prosthetic. I untied my arm tube and pretended to be high, easy to do for a former junkie like me. "Good skag, man."

Johnny went next. His face tensed before he pierced his arm then relaxed. He turned hooded eyes to Nevada. Her hands shook as she tapped a vein and braced the slender stem of the needle to her skin. The three of us watched her, waiting. Her upper teeth dug into her lip. She broke the skin and depressed the plunger. As the poison entered her system, her face went slack, limbs dropping to her side, knees buckling.

Took everything I had to stay in my seat and not catch her. I catch Nevada. It's my purpose. Instead, Johnny wrapped an arm around her hips and tugged her into his lap. "You good?" He didn't seem high, he seemed worried as hell.

She whimpered, her forehead falling to his chest.

The choice on my shoulders weighed a ton. Close the deal and watch Nevada get arrested or call it off.

She raised her head, pressed her lips to Johnny's, and started making out with him. He kissed her back, hesitantly. Still worried. It hit me like a mortar blast. The sinking feeling like you're drowning and no one is coming to save you. The unbearable loss that paralyzes you and zaps your will to breathe. I'd lost Nev to drugs like I'd lost her parents. Opioids had taken everything of value to me, time and time again. The unwinnable battle I foolishly kept fighting.

Consumed with grief, my thinking clouded, I made a decision that would affect Nev for the rest of her life.

I handed Darin the envelope and grabbed the brick. "It's been a pleasure doing business with you."

The room exploded with agents dressed in black battle gear. "FBI. Freeze. Hands up."

Darin raised his hands slowly, smart enough not to reach for a weapon. My coworkers cuffed him first, rifles trained on Johnny and me.

My partner, Tavian, cuffed Johnny, who didn't fight back and still didn't seem high. His gaze narrowed on Nevada as they held her hands behind her back.

She swayed, the whites of her eyes rolling up. I reached for her, but there was too much distance and too many people between us. "Catch her!"

My yell died in the chaos. She fell forward, her head making a sickening clunk on the table before she landed on the ground, on her side, eyes closed, mouth open.

"Nev!"

She didn't move. Fuck! That shit could kill her. With all my force, I shoved two agents out of the way. A strong arm around my neck halted my progress. "Chill." I recognized Special Agent Hawkster's harsh whisper in my ear. "Don't blow it now."

I could overpower him easily, but he outranked me. He was also a mean sonofabitch. He'd make my life hell if I didn't comply. I stepped back and watched helplessly as several members of the tag team rushed to help her, one of them female.

As Agent Hawkster ushered me out the back door, I arched my neck to catch a glimpse of the bottom of her shoes, fanned out at an awkward angle. "Narcan! Give her Narcan." They needed to administer the anti-overdose drug quickly. It could save her life.

Hawkster yanked my arms up, forcing me to bend forward and sending shooting pain to my shoulders. "Check yourself, Capioni. They know what they're doing."

In the alley, they placed Darin and Johnny in separate cars. Hawkster walked me to a third vehicle and pushed my shoulder, forcing me to sit. If he wasn't my supervisor, I'd flatten him.

"What the hell is your problem? I don't care what that girl means to you, you do not compromise an operation, and you do not drop cover. Ever."

Shit. I fucked up. I lowered my head. "I need to get back to her."

An ambulance tore out of the alley, sirens flashing and blaring.

"She just left. You get driven to the field office, anyone watching sees you've been "arrested." You're free to go once Aquino is secure. Follow procedure." He slammed the car door shut, leaving me alone and hand-cuffed in the back of an FBI vehicle.

I fell against the seat. Procedure. God, I fucking hated procedure.

Tavian opened the door. "She's the Nevada you've been looking for?"

"Yes." I sighed.

"She's fucking beautiful." He shook his head.

"She sure is. Now help me get to her."

With his hand on the roof of the vehicle, he scanned the area. He leaned in to whisper, "I'll spring you from detention at the field office. Then I'll help you find her."

He left and I sat waiting and helpless, back where I started, searching in the dark for Nevada.

Chapter 2

Lachlan

At the Boston field office, Agent Hawkster led me to a holding room. He removed my cuffs and reached for the door. "Stay here."

"No."

He looked back at me, his eyes tight. If he made me wait any longer, I'd lose it. My job be damned. "I need to get to her. What happened to the girl?"

He held his phone to his ear and raised his palm. "Where's the girl from tonight's bust? Mass Gen?"

Tavian appeared in the doorway, his face serious, voice formal. "Aquino's secure. Let's go, Cutlass."

Hawkster nodded and moved aside. "She's in the ER at Mass Gen."

"Thank you." I raced down the corridor, Tavian at my back.

"Take the east exit," he called.

I stopped and headed east at the next hallway.

"That's west, Lefty."

He chuckled at me as I spun and ran the other way.

"I'm in a hurry, alright. East, west, north, fuck it all to hell."

We made it to his Corvette, hopped in, and tore out of the lot.

He didn't say anything, but his lips pressed together and he snuck a glance at me to see if I was watching him.

"Aquino wasn't secure yet, was he?" I asked him.

"Fuck no. If you kept going "east" you woulda run right past him."

Nothing in hell would make me laugh right now, but I appreciated his attempt.

Nevada's brother, Colt, answered my call on the first ring. "Detective Colt Lacy."

"Brace yourself." Was there a good way to deliver this news? Colt's mental state had been deteriorating during our search. Lately every death he encountered at work seemed to bring him deeper into a black abyss.

"Talk, fucker."

"I found Nevada. She's at Mass Gen ER." I was still breathing hard from the run.

"Shit. What's her condition?"

I gritted my teeth and tried to calm my voice. Didn't want to hurt Colt, ever. Never wanted to bring him bad news again. "Things went bad during an op. She shot up heroin and passed out. My handler forced me out... I couldn't see... Hoping like fuck they got Narcan in her system in time."

"On my way."

Five minutes later, Tavian fishtailed into the ambulance access area at Mass Gen. I raced through the doors and ran to the desk. "Where's Nevada Lacy?"

Three nurses approached me. One of them I knew from Siege. *Devin*. I'd never fucked Devin, but we'd spent a few nights talking. I think she thought it might go farther, but she didn't turn me on. Too sweet. No fire. Not Nevada.

"I need to see Nevada Lacy. Where is she?"

"Let me check the records."

What the hell? No time for fucking records. I brushed past the nurses' station and charged down the hall to the ER. "Nev!" Every damn bay was either empty or not her.

"You can't enter there." Devin trailed far behind me.

"Nev! I need Nevada Lacy!" Where the fuck was she? I didn't see any cops, no security. Did Aquino get to her?

I stopped dead in my tracks when the last person I expected to see blocked my path.

Johnny Blanco.

Fuck me. Nevada's "man."

"What the everlovin' hell are you doin' here?"

"Could say the same of you." He stepped toward me, shoulders high, face pissed, ready to fight.

Good. I was looking for a fight right about now. No. I was looking for Nevada.

"Where is she? Is she in there?" I'd have to throw down with Johnny later. I needed to find her.

"She..."

Fuck him and whatever he had to say. I yanked the curtain aside. God, she looked terrible. Sunken eyes, a tube in her nose, her makeup smeared, hair a rat's nest. "Nev."

Her hands felt cold and sweaty. The nurses and Johnny followed me into the room. I placed my palms on her cheeks, trying to give her some warmth. "Nev. It's me. Lachlan."

Her eyes fluttered and she moaned.

"She doesn't give a fuck who you are. She's high." Johnny Blanco needed to shut his trap.

I spun on him. "Because of you. You got her hooked on drugs?"

Johnny took a step back and held up his hands. He bumped into Colt's chest as he entered the room. Johnny turned around and came face to shield with a Boston PD badge. Colt outweighed him by a good fifty pounds and had at least six inches on him.

"You turned her into an addict?" Colt sucker punched him in the jaw and knocked him to the ground. "That's my little sister, you loser." Colt dropped to his knees and slugged Johnny in the face again.

Johnny reacted slowly, probably still high. Odd because he didn't look high at all. In fact, he never reacted to the heroin he shot in his arm. They arrested him with me and released him...

Loud clicks filled my brain as all the pieces came together. *Click. Click. Click.* "He's a cop!"

Johnny flipped Colt to his back and straddled him. He didn't throw a punch, but lay his torso over Colt, pinning his wrists beside his head.

"You're a cop and you got her high?" Colt's face twisted, his breathing harsh.

Johnny released Colt's hands and sat up. "DEA. And I didn't get her high. She did it to keep her cover. I didn't want her to."

Goddamn. I ran my hands through my hair. "Let him up."

Johnny helped Colt up. They brushed off their clothes as they stared each other.

I offered my hand to Johnny. "FBI. Lachlan Cutlass."

He took my hand and gave it a cautious shake. "Johnny Slade Boudreaux. Go by Slade."

"That's Colt Lacy, her brother. Boston PD."

"Sorry." Colt rubbed the back of his neck and avoided eye contact with Johnny/Slade.

A thousand clicks sounded in my head, all at once. "Nevada was undercover for the DEA?"

"Nevada and I were under Aquino."

"For eight months? I bought from you." How many deals had I done with Johnny Blanco? At least twelve. "You had plenty of evidence to nail him."

"We were holding out for a link to Greco. We had a meet set up with Tyler Gunderson." Johnny spoke under his breath, glancing at Colt.

Trying to get Greco, the Mafia capo, through his consigliere? Holy shit.

"Greco killed our parents." The muscles in Colt's neck grew tight and his fists shook.

Johnny focused on Colt's face then checked the corridor. The room needed to be cleared before we talked about the case, but with emotions running high, we all let protocol slip. He stepped closer to Colt and whispered, "I'm aware. The DEA is not. We were close. The FBI just threw away all the work her and I put in."

I didn't bother to whisper. No way I could keep my voice down now. What the hell were they thinking? "Going after Greco through Gunderson has got to be the stupidest plan I've ever heard. Who came up with that shit? You need an army to take down Greco, not little Nevada dressed up like a junkie." They'd bitten off way more than they should, took too many risks, and she got hurt.

"Little Nevada?" Slade laughed and looked down at his feet as they shuffled on the floor. When he spoke again, his tone was more reticent. "You don't know her at all."

"I know her. I know she's way too young and way too close to this case to make any life-threatening judgement calls."

"If you're so close, why didn't she tell you she'd taken a job with the DEA?" Slade raised his chin.

He had me there. She kept a huge secret from me. Colt too. She quit her job years ago and took this position and didn't tell us? Why?

Colt walked to her bed, his face drawn. At least she was sleeping through the worst part. Being awake during a bad trip was a bus ride to hell. I'd experienced it a few times and never wanted that for her.

Slade stepped to the other side of her bed. "You shot up too. Prosthetic?" he asked me.

"Yeah. Why didn't she have one?" I returned.

"We were under too deep. We couldn't risk meeting a makeup artist to apply the prosthetic. I used a rubber ball in my elbow. Aquino was watching Nevada like a hawk. She couldn't pull off a fake."

"Doctor Christensen is here. Please step back." A nurse entered the room and motioned for us to move away from the bed. A female doctor entered behind the nurse. About five-foot-nine, long brown hair, mid-thirties. "Call me Dr. Darby." She strode directly to Nevada. Her forehead crinkled and moved as she checked Nevada's chart, her pulse, and her temperature. She raised the bandage on her forehead and replaced it. "Nevada. Can you squeeze my hand? Squeeze my hand."

Nevada's fingertip moved ever so slightly. Colt glanced at me and back at her. Her finger moved and she had a smart, compassionate doctor. The first positive signs since I'd arrived.

Dr. Darby's gaze passed from Slade to Colt to me. "Are you her family?"

"Yes." All three of us answered.

Her lips turned down in a skeptical frown. "Mr. Blanco filled me in on her situation and how she came to inject the heroin into her system. Luckily, the FBI team administered Narcan in time to prevent death from overdose."

Excellent. I owed my team huge gratitude.

"Her breathing and blood pressure are still dangerously low. The contusion on her head has significant swelling. We'll keep her overnight. If she does well, we can send her home, or she can go to a rehab center to get through the withdrawals, but she'll need to be watched twenty-four seven."

"No rehab center," I said.

"She won't be alone." Colt reassured the doctor.

"She has all three of us." Slade got the last word.

"Me too." Tavian poked his head into the room. He'd never even met Nevada, but I talked about her enough he knew how much I cared for her.

Dr. Darby laughed at us jockeying for position to help Nevada, but we all wanted to be the one to be there for her.

"If she wakes, she'll be disoriented and paranoid. Don't stress her. She needs to focus on rest and recovery." We all nodded, but tension filled the tiny space. "In fact, I'm placing an order of one person at a time in this room."

Darn, Dr. Darby figured us out fast and set a rule to keep us in line. Oh well, rules were meant to be broken because I wasn't leaving Nevada for anything. "I'll go first." I grabbed a chair and set it down at the foot of her bed.

"I'm staying." Colt pulled up the other chair in the room and sat down three feet away from me. He crossed his arms over his chest. "Try to move me."

Dr. Darby laughed again because Colt was huge.

Slade left the area and came back with a chair. "We all stay."

"I could call security..." Dr. Darby's smile didn't fade.

"We are the security," Colt answered her.

True. Nev would be well guarded by a cop, an FBI agent, and a DEA agent.

Tavian waved. "I'm out. I'll cover for you, Cutlass."

I nodded and leaned back in my chair. Good to have Tavian on my side. Guess we were all staying.

Chapter 3

———

We sat in silence in the private room they'd moved Nevada into just before midnight. My adrenaline ebbed with each rise and fall of her chest. The uninterrupted beeping of her heart monitor became a sentinel in the chaos of my mind.

Three in the morning, I called Rogan. "We found her."

"She alright?"

I'd probably woken him, but a sniper never sleeps deep. "She's injured." Even though I could trust Rogan, the details of the case had to remain confidential. Colt was another story, he needed to know, but not Rogan. "She'll recover."

"Glad to hear it. Keep me posted."

"Will do."

Sitting in this room, watching Nev fight for her life, almost losing her, actually losing her for eight months, the simmering need to tell Colt my secret boiled over. The unspoken truth hiding between us since our teens all came to a head in this hospital room. Worst case, I'd lose the only close friend I'd ever had. Best case, I'd become his brother-in-law.

I decided not to wait for Slade to leave the room. He needed to be made aware too. Deflate any hopes he had of being with her.

"I gotta tell you both something."

They snapped out of their half-sleeping state and turned their heads my way.

"I love her."

Slade looked away. "Fuck."

Colt's tired eyes went blank. "Bullshit."

"Always have."

"You're lying." This was Colt. I liked to prank him, but now was not the time.

"I'm not. She loves me too."

"Aww, hell." Slade leaned forward in his chair and stared at me. "My understanding is you haven't seen her in eight months."

"That's why I've been looking for her for eight months." If he did have feelings for her, he would not win this one.

"She's been my girl for those eight months, my partner for two years before that. You got no claim to her." He stood and turned away from me. Slade was tall and buff. Nev might be attracted to him, but he didn't stand a chance against me. She'd given me plenty of hints over the years, all I had to do was make a move and she'd be mine.

"Being under as your girl is not the same as really being your girl. Don't confuse the two. She's your partner. I'm sure you've got a friendship built, but it's nothing like what we got."

"Oh yeah? We'll see about that."

Colt sat silent and still while I talked to Slade. He appeared calm on the outside. Didn't mean a storm wasn't brewing.

"I'm telling you where I'm at. If you guys got a problem with it, we can address it now, but it's not going away."

Colt finally spoke. "How'd this come about?"

"It hasn't yet. Officially. It's just somethin' I've known for a while and didn't act on. She was only sixteen. I was eighteen. She was my best friend's little sister, grieving the brutal murders of both her parents. All through college, I watched over her. Drove her home when she drank too much. We talked late at night, shared our hopes and dreams, fell in love... I did shit about it. She gave up on waiting on me and got a boyfriend. I joined the Navy. I waited too long. Done waiting now."

"Damn it, Cutlass. You were her other brother." Colt finally let some anger show. That's fine. I wanted to hash this out.

"We were never brother and sister. Not after your parents died. You and me are still brothers. But her, no. Want her to be my wife, not my sister."

He shook his head and stood up. "Damn it all to hell." He slammed his fist into the wall. The echo bounced through the room.

Nevada flinched and whimpered. Her eyes opened, and her torso rose like a mummy from the dead. She looked around, but her eyes didn't focus. She pushed away the sheets, jumped off the bed—breaking off her IV and oxygen tubes—and crouched on the floor, her arms around her knees. "I'm dead."

We all took cautious steps toward her. She looked like a frightened child cornered by coyotes in an alley. Blood dripped from the IV insertion point in her arm.

"Nev." Colt used a calm voice that came from great strength and years of practice on the police force. I couldn't summon calmness now.

Her gaze flitted around, but didn't stop on anything in the room. She was in her head, not here. "They're in the house. They shot me. I'm dead. Tell Colt."

Oh god. She was reliving the trauma of her mother's murder.

"I'm Colt. I'm here, Nev." His voice was tortured.

Her body broke into tremors. "Tell Lachlan I'm dead. Tell him my mom's bleeding in the kitchen. Tell him to send help."

The pain of that night slammed into my chest again as if I were reliving it too. I should've stayed with her and her mom after her father's memorial service. Instead I let her convince Colt and me to compete in an evening swim meet. She said her dad would want me to win the championship my senior year. I won, but I'd give it all up to have been there when Luigi Greco's men broke in the house, killed her mother, and shot Nev's shoulder. Thank god she had the wits to pretend to be dead.

Colt reached for her arm, but she flinched away. She considered Slade for a second. Her attention bounced up to Colt, then stopped on me.

"Lachlan." My name came out like a desperate plea.

"Yes, baby. I'm here."

Colt backed up, making room for me to approach her.

"I'm here."

Our eyes met. Pinpoint pupils under hooded eyelids found me and recognized me. For the first time tonight, my Nev looked at me and saw me. "My mom..." Her voice turned up, asking me for reassurance her mom was still alive.

I couldn't lie to her and tell her it would be okay. Just like that night, I had to give her the truth. "Your mom's gone."

Her face scrunched up. "I know."

"Yeah." I took a few steps closer to her.

"Catch me." Her eyes closed and her head fell to the side. I had her off the floor and in my lap in seconds, me sitting on her hospital bed, her head tucked under my chin.

"I caught you, Nev."

She whimpered a painful cry. "I have the flu."

"No, baby. You're detoxing after taking heroin."

"I am? That sucks." She slurred into my chest.

"You're gonna be okay, Nev. You'll get through this."

Her fingernails scraped at my shirt like she wanted to crawl inside me. With a sigh, her hand went limp.

I looked up to see Slade and Colt watching us, their faces locked in shock at the rawness of what just happened.

My heart pounded like I'd run five miles. Nevada was in agony. But we'd connected, and she knew I caught her. So we'd crossed the starting line. Not sure how many more miles we had to go, but we'd taken the first step.

Slade's shoulders hunched forward. "I'll go get the nurse."

Nevada's flashback smacked him over the head with the proof he need-ed. First thing when she woke, scared and confused, she asked for me. Not him. She didn't ask about the case. She called out for me to catch her. She didn't tell him directly she loved me, but *my* name came out of her mouth first. Didn't surprise me, but Slade needed time.

Colt lowered his head and ran his hands over his head. "Fuck man, that was heavy."

"Go get the nurse with Slade. I got her."

He nodded and walked out. I kissed Nev on the top of her head. "Don't worry. I'm here. I'm not leaving. I'll catch you. I'll hold you. Not giving up on you. You need strength, take mine. Whatever you need, babe, take it from me now."

Her fingers squeezed ever so slightly at my waist. Weak, but still there. Still with me.

Chapter 4

"I have to go fill out paperwork." Slade stood from his chair after finishing a seven a.m. call with his supervisor. "What should I tell them?"

Tell them the FBI screwed up. Tell them Lachlan Cutlass blew it. Again. "Leave out the part where she woke up last night. Everything else? The truth. Both agencies recorded it."

Slade nodded, touched Nev's hand, and left.

"It's like incest, dude." Colt hadn't talked about it in front of Slade, but the second he left, I guess he'd decided to share how he felt.

"It's nothing like incest. Trust me." I had to smile thinking about her red hair sweeping the floor when she hangs upside down in her yoga swing. Her perfectly round breasts, fighting gravity to stay in her sports bra.

"Ew. Are you fucking my sister?"

The coffee I was drinking sputtered out with my laugh. "No. God, Colt. Did you have to go straight there?" My hand swept across my beard. Needed to shave this thing if the case was over. "We're not fucking. We're not anything. We never have. Plan to change that though as soon as she's better."

He grimaced. Colt and I had been friends a long time. Best friends. We'd make it through me loving his sister, just like we'd made it through everything.

"So you know you love her but you haven't done it yet?" He kept his eyes on her sleeping form as he sipped his coffee.

Colt made his decisions with his dick. He wouldn't even date a girl until he'd fucked her three times to make sure they were compatible. "Yes. That is possible, you know."

"So how do you know you love her?"

Colt and I never went too deep on the subject of love. I'd be exposing another part of my soul to him if I told him, but I could trust Colt. He'd proven that many times over. "How do you know you're breathing? You feel it in your lungs. It's natural, it's right, it's good, and it's exciting. The way each hello and goodbye feels like the last time and the first time, the way she looks at me like I'm a fucking hero, the secrets we've shared late at night while we're holding onto each other. We've been apart a lot, but when we're together, destiny takes over. My heart rate shoots through the roof, my lungs suck her in like I just ran forty miles."

"Enough!" Colt held up a hand to stop me. "Enough. I get it."

I chuckled because we'd have to redefine the limits of guy talk around his sister. "Anyway, nothing like incest."

"I'll need some time."

"I get that. But trust me, you don't need to worry. In all the years you've known me, have you ever seen me chase after a girl? No. They always come to me. I'm not bragging and I admit I indulged every once in a while, but none of them really turned me on. All these years, only one woman ever turned me on. It's always been her."

⸺⸺⸺⸺⸺⸺

AN HOUR LATER, SHE popped up in the bed, looked around, and made a mad dash for the bathroom. Luckily, they'd removed the oxygen and IV after she woke up earlier. Colt and I ran into the bathroom behind her. I caught her hair right before she vomited into the toilet.

The nurse came in. "Excuse me." We stepped back, and she helped her wash her face, use the toilet, and return to the bed. She checked her vitals. "How're you feeling?"

"Thirsty."

The nurse helped her drink some water.

"Burning hot, achy like someone punched me."

"That's normal. Dr. Darby has prescribed an optional medication that will help reduce the withdrawal symptoms. It's called Lofexidine. Would you like to take that?"

"Yes."

I didn't like the desperation in her tone. I'd heard it coming from my own mouth and I knew. Desperation to make the pain go away led people to use again. Coming down from heroin hurt more than any other drug, but she had to get through it. I'd help her.

"I'll be right back. Try to stay awake till I return."

Nevada nodded, and her gaze flitted from her brother to me. Her pupils still pinpoints, no recognition showed in her eyes. She yawned. "I'm so tired."

"Wait till the nurse gives you the medication. Then you can sleep again." Colt seemed happy to be back in his role of telling her what to do.

The nurse returned, and Nevada was able to take the pill with a sip of water. "I hope that helps, honey."

The nurse handed me a bedpan and a wet cloth. "You can wipe her forehead with this. Try to keep her calm."

I stepped up to her side and pressed the cloth to her temple. "You're doing great, Nev. You're almost there. This is the worst part."

"There's spiderwebs on my legs."

"I know. They'll be gone soon."

NEVADA WOKE UP FOUR hours later. Eleven in the morning. "Get away from me."

Colt and I both stared at her in shock. We'd been holding vigil and she'd barely spoken. Now her eyes were wide, her voice loud and clear.

"Johnny!" She screamed out the door. "Johnny, help me. Help me, Johnny!"

Colt stepped up to her with his palm up to calm her in the same way he'd approach a spooked horse.

"Stay back." Her hands skimmed the bed. She grabbed her call button and pointed it at Colt. "Hands up!"

I still had my beard, so I understood if she didn't recognize me or thought I was Lake Capioni, but her brother?

"Nev. It's me, Colt. That's Lachlan. We won't hurt you."

"I know who the fuck you are. I hate you both! Get Johnny."

"Or what? You gonna kill me with that call button?"

She looked at her hands for a second, then dropped the button. Her face crumbled like she wanted to cry. "Where's Johnny?"

"Johnny is Slade, and he's at the DEA field office filling out paperwork," I answered her.

"You know he's Slade?" This made her irrationally sad.

The drugs were still messing with her, so I kept my voice steady. "Yes, and I know you were undercover with the DEA."

"What were you doing there, Lachlan?"

"I'm FBI now. I was there to bust Aquino. You were a shock."

"Did you leave the SEALs?"

"Yeah, when you went missing, I turned down my renewal and retired. You scared the shit outta me, girl."

"You were undercover too? It all happened so fast, but I didn't believe you were there to buy drugs. You wouldn't do that." Her mouth twisted in pain.

"We can talk about all this later. Right now, just get through this. You're coming down from the heroin."

She stared at me like I was the devil. "You knew I was undercover and you still let the FBI bust me?"

"No. I didn't know until later. I thought you were a junkie."

"You thought I was a junkie and you still busted me?" The pain of betrayal filled her voice.

Shit. She had me there. "Yes."

"Fuck you, Lachlan. Fuck Lake Capioni. Fuck the FBI for screwing up my op and blowing my cover."

"I understand you're mad, but your cover's not blown. Aquino thinks you and Johnny were arrested too. He doesn't know who the rat was."

"Good. Hopefully he thinks it was you!" She pointed a finger at me. "So Johnny and I can go back in and get Greco."

"You are not going back under for Greco."

"The hell I'm not."

"Nevada." Colt stepped close and grabbed her hand. "Calm down. Let's get the drugs out of your system, and then we'll talk about the case."

She broke his hold and threw up her hands. "Oh my god! Does the DEA know I shot up?"

"They know. FBI and DEA recorded the whole thing." Colt gave her the bad news.

"My career is over." She fell back into the pillow and pressed her palms to her eyes.

"Not necessarily. Hey, speaking of career. What the hell, Nevada? You go and join the DEA and you don't tell your brother or me?"

"Fuck you."

Alrighty. This was not the romantic reunion I was expecting. Apparently crashing from heroin brought out the bitch in Nevada.

"You got something to say for yourself? You quit your job, went through Quantico, and didn't tell either one of us anything that was going on? Like we didn't matter? You didn't expect us to freak out and come look for you when you fell off the grid? You didn't think I'd go crazy combing the streets looking for you every second of every day? Of course I would, and Colt would too. We'd do anything for you, and you blew us off and went undercover with *Johnny* and now you're asking for Johnny like he's somebody. He's nobody. He's shit on my shoe." Colt held up his hand, trying to stop me. Not happening. "Colt is your brother, and I'm your man. You deal with us."

"You are not my man!" she said, insulted. "You are a controlling, overbearing, overprotective, big brother who's actually *not* a big brother who disappears every six months and reappears when he wants, leaving me behind to pick up the pieces. So excuse me if I didn't put my life on hold and tell you every detail, of which you wouldn't approve anyway. Excuse me for going after what I want when I knew you wouldn't support me."

"I supported you." My voice broke. How could she say I didn't support her? Everything I did was for her.

"You did not. Neither one of you did. I talked about it all the time. Anytime I mentioned the DEA, you shut me down. *It's too dangerous. Quantico is too hard. You're too idealistic. You don't have the tactical skills. Revenge won't bring them back.* Meanwhile you and Colt are out getting vengeance on the world while I'm sitting here with a desk job at the Port Authority. I'm not allowed to fight back for all the things that happened to me? Why? Because I'm a poor little girl? No. Don't talk to me about support. Just leave me alone and get me Johnny." She turned to her side and clutched the pillow, looking about to break into tears again.

"Fine. I'll get you Slade. If he's who you want. Bye, Nevada."

Fuck her and her heroin and her lies and her stubborn goddamn insults. I stormed out of the hospital to my truck.

Colt followed me. "This is so fucked up."

"She's mad at *us*! All I did was try to save her." I gave up my military career *for her*. Shit, I sat there and put myself on the chopping block in front of Colt and Slade *for her*, and she woke up and sliced my head off.

"She's telling us she didn't want to be saved." Colt shook his head. "I had no idea she felt this strongly about the DEA. She'd mentioned it, and I did blow her off. Gotta say I'm impressed as hell she made it through training and kept it from us for years."

"I'll be impressed after I'm done being pissed." I opened my truck, which Tavian had dropped off, and climbed into the driver's seat. Not sitting around in an old hospital chair for her any longer. "I'll send Slade over right now, check in with the office, cool my jets, and be back tonight. Call me if her condition changes."

With one hand on the roof, he leaned into my cab. "She's still a mess. Give her some time." He could try to put a positive spin on this but his eyes and mouth held worry and doubt.

"Heroin is like truth serum. That's how she really feels about me? Overprotective? Abandoning her for my own agenda? I fucking thought I loved her. I was so wrong."

"We'll sort it out. Go get your shit done." He didn't spout any more fake optimism at me. It was useless.

"Right. Later."

He tapped the top of my truck as I closed my door. The engine rumbled to life, and I left the lot without looking back at the hospital. No trying to see her room from the lot like I'd normally do.

Damn Nevada and Colt and Slade. Screw them all to hell.

Chapter 5

———

Nevada

Colt forced me to go home with Lachlan. Ignored my protests and decided Lachlan would be the one to take me home. To his house. Not mine. His. In the end, I gave in to their pressure. I'd lose my cover if Aquino found me at my old apartment, and I needed time to recover before going back to the hole-in-the-wall Slade and I had stayed in for the op. Colt had to work, and Lachlan took the day off for me. Swallowing my pride, I climbed in his truck and he shut my door.

All Lachlan's perfection hit me as he walked around the back, folded in, and started the engine of his Ford F150 Raptor. Spotless floor mats protected his black carpet, all the chrome shined, big tires lifted us high off the ground. His manly hand wrapped around the gearshift between us. The floor mats in my old Honda were stained, and my wipers made semi-circular dirt treads on the front windshield.

After I took in his truck, his profile caught my eye. His forehead was so strong and determined, like he could charge a rhino and win the battle. His nose and jaw tapered to tantalizing points, and his plush lips curved in an adorable smile at some secret joke in his head. Darn him for distracting me from my anger. Now that he'd shaved the beard and cut his hair, I recognized him as the man I knew, my brother's best friend, my friend. But his face also reflected maturity he'd earned while he served as a SEAL. His high-stress deployments aged him and gave his eyes a few wrinkles any other thirty-two-year-old man wouldn't have yet. But he wore them well. Really well.

Flawless Lachlan. The beautiful itch I could never scratch. One, because he had no interest in me that way. When my dad brought him home one night and said we were taking him in, I was an awkward teen with frizzy red hair, pimples, and a few extra pounds. Even though I'd grown and changed, he still saw me as that girl.

And second, because he took his role as my brother's best friend way too seriously. Sure he'd drive me home when I'd had too much to drink, but he also told me I couldn't do things. That's why I joined up with the DEA without telling him. Quantico was hard enough without him intimidating me.

Ironically, below my skin, a real itch also haunted me. An itch that moved and teased, never to be eased, no matter how deep my fingernails dug into my skin.

I always knew drugs killed, now I'd lived it. Heroin was a walking death. Forty-eight hours later, and I still felt lost. I could understand why so many first-time users went back and did it again. The short-lived rush of incredible warmth made me happier than I'd ever felt. Nothing bad could reach me there. But the pain now, I'd do anything to have that high again and get rid of this, even for a little while.

"You okay?" His voice. God, his voice, over the music on his radio. Deep, gravelly, sexy, sweet, distracting me from the itch at the same time reminding me of it.

"I should stay with Slade." My fingernails raked over my skin again, which was red and dry from all the scratching. "My cover—"

"Your cover is intact. Aquino's in custody."

Another ten minutes, and he pulled his truck into the drive of a one-story house in Chelsea.

"He won't find us here. I have a surprise for you."

"Not sure I can handle any more surprises after the last two days." Shooting heroin for the first time and Lachlan showing up with the FBI at my undercover op were quite enough, thank you.

"It'll bring you back to you." His voice was nicer than I deserved after I yelled at him earlier today. One of the many things I loved about Lachlan, he didn't stay mad for long. His smile always mended any torn threads.

The cold air outside made a foggy mist collect on my window. I wiped it away with my hand to see the steps up to the porch. "I don't know who I am anymore."

He hummed in agreement. "Undercover work does that to you. Same with combat and extended deployments. Friends who are enemies. Your life on the line with every move. Waiting five months for five minutes of action. You can lose yourself fast." He knew me. Lachlan knew all my weaknesses. "No organism can live in a constant state of stress. We need that recovery time. You were under too long. It's time to decompress. I'll help you. C'mon."

I pulled my coat tight, and he slung an arm around my shoulders as we walked to the front door. I felt safe tucked into his side. He clicked on the light, and a thumping, buzzing, energy came at me full speed. My Samoyed, Shanti, whimpered, and a giant fluff of white bounded to me, his weight hitting my chest. I dropped to my knees and wrapped my arms around his wiggling neck. "Shanti! I missed you so much." His wet tongue lapped at my face, his tail swinging hard. "How are you, boy?" He knocked me onto my butt and I laughed, holding onto his neck and rubbing his head.

"He's spoiled rotten now. When he's not on one of his three walks a day, he's lounging on the porch or in his luxury doggy bed." Lachlan pointed to a giant dog bed in the living room.

"Here? You've been watching Shanti?" When I said his name, he broke into a full repeat of all the excitement of our reunion.

"Yep. Crystal's great and everything, but he thought he'd been abandoned. He knows if he's with me, you'll be there soon. He needed a yard, so I bought this place."

"This is your house?" Lachlan always had apartments so he could easily leave on his missions. For many years, he lived in a trailer he stored in Colt's backyard. Massive old weeping willows shaded the expanse of lawn in front of this house. The kind of trees you could hang a swing on. The kind of trees kids could climb.

"You like it?" He grabbed a stuffed duck and tossed it for Shanti who happily clomped on the hardwood floors into a massive living room. On his way back, I noticed the furniture was modern and spotless, like his truck. Everything was covered in white. No splashes of color or personality. Add a woman's touch and the room would be fantastic.

"You met Crystal?"

"I met all the women from your gym. Checked in with them weekly. They missed you too."

Odd. Lachlan and I had been friends, good friends. He'd helped me through some rough times, but we'd always kept certain parts of our lives separate. Like my friends at the gym. He'd never walked my dog for me.

"Thank you." I couldn't keep the wonder out of my voice. This was all too surreal. Regret for the mean words I said to Lachlan flooded me. I shouldn't have yelled at him. I held equal responsibility for the mess we found ourselves in. I'd kept secrets from him, and he acted out of concern for me.

"How you feeling?"

He must've seen my brain struggling with all this. "Tired. Antsy. Hungry."

"Let's have some food, and you can sleep while I take Shanti out for a run."

"Okay." I took off my jacket and shoes and left them on a rack in the foyer. Lachlan took off his coat but kept his shoes on.

"Your clothes are in the master bedroom closet."

"They are?"

"I thought you'd like to have your stuff around you."

He spent a good amount of time thinking about what I'd want today. "I would."

"Toiletries too. That expensive green shit you buy."

Even bathroom supplies. "You brought my Sage Cream? My skin. It will feel..."

"Better."

"Bedroom is at the end of the hall." He pointed to the hallway off the living room. Following his directions led me to a gorgeous master bedroom. My heart thumped in my chest. This room had a woman's touch. In fact, it had *my* touch. My velvety bedspread in pearlized seafoam green and my shaggy white pillows covered the bed. My toes dug into the plush rugs under my feet, the green leaves and silver threads in my favorite colors. He'd brought them here from my place.

Along the wall, recessed lighting glowed down on a stunning built-in bookshelf. The light through the glass shelves cast a luminous aura over the neatly-aligned books, like they floated magically on the wall. They glowed behind a plush rocker set in front of them for the sole purpose of reading. A fantasy book corner.

I stepped closer and glanced at the titles.

Danielle Steel, Kristen Ashley, Twilight, Harry Potter.

Oh my gosh. These were *my* books. I ran my fingers over the spines, letting the words seep from their pages and through my skin into my soul. When I felt empty, nothing filled me up like escaping in a book.

I felt his presence behind me. I turned to see him leaning against the door jamb and smiling at me like he enjoyed watching me discover all the work he'd done. "I was at your place, collecting a few things, and I realized you might like to have your books. So I built the bookshelf for you."

"Um, wow. It's stunning. Really. And it does make me feel better to have them here. Thank you."

He nodded, knocked on the wall, and walked out.

In the shower, my favorite Sage lavender oils and tea tree lotion felt so good. Puzzle pieces swam around in my foggy mind, struggling to fit it all together.

Lachlan moved my clothes, my dog, my HABA (what I called my health and beauty aids), and my library into his house. My most personal possessions. And the things I missed the most about my life before I went undercover.

Certainly it must be temporary. He couldn't expect me to live here, could he? With him? I slipped into my old PJs. Simple black boy shorts and a rainbow tie-dyed tee with shredded sleeves. My face looked pale and skinny, my hair dark. I found a hair tie and piled my wet hair on my head. He'd brought my makeup too so I put on mascara, but nothing else. Lachlan had seen me at my worst many times, and he was still my friend. A friend who was acting exceptionally friendly.

I'm your man.

Bizarre. I thought I heard him say *I'm your man*. Damn heroin had me believing in some stupid hallucination. My brain did that to me even without drugs in my system. It blended fantasy and reality. I swear I lived in an alternate universe where bad guys could be vampires and good guys could be wizards. Lachlan was simply overcompensating for ruining my op, and he was doing it in his own over-the-top way.

I came out of the bathroom, and my heart melted at Shanti waiting on the rug for me like he always used to do. "Hi, boy." Sometimes you take for granted your dog waiting for you to come out of the shower. It's not until you're away from him for a while that you really miss it. You open the shower door, and there's no one waiting. But Shanti was here. His smiling face, his wagging tail, and his cute little nose smiling up at me like I was his whole world. He'd forgiven me for abandoning him, and we were back together again, a team.

Lachlan knocked at the door. "Brought you some grub."

He entered the room looking adorable with a wooden tray arranged with strawberries, dark chocolate, and tiny wedges of white and orange cheese. Hardly grub. It looked delicious and so did he with the quirky smile he had on his lips. Was he nervous?

He set the tray on the end of the bed and pulled up a chair. I sat on the bed and took a strawberry.

"You feeling better?"

"Yeah. Not all the way yet, but on the way."

"Good."

A weird silence filled the room. He watched me eat another strawberry. I tried not to stare at him, but he looked hot as hell in his faded blue jeans and the maroon Henley he was wearing. He had the top buttons open, a few chest hairs peeking out.

I held in my sigh. I always ached for Lachlan, but he'd never done more than hold me. He was a great cuddler when I cried, but other than that, well... except for the one kiss before he left for BUD/S training. That kiss was everything to me. And nothing to him.

Lachlan grabbed a strawberry from the tray and held it up to my lips.

My eyes crossed as I stared at it. "What?"

"Take a bite."

Lachlan wanted to feed me strawberries? Now I'd clearly gone round the bend. But hell, okay.

I leaned forward and took a bite. How come the strawberry from his hand tasted so much better than the one I ate seconds ago?

His eyes grew hungry as he watched my lips. He needed to eat too. God, if only that hunger was for me. We could be... something. But he didnt see me that way. I was the best-friend's kid sister. He didn't see me as a woman.

He tilted his chin and his gorgeous blue eyes pinned mine to the spot. "I'd like to take you on a date."

Did I hear him right?

The strawberry stuck in my throat, and I coughed a loud obnoxious cough. He did not say what I thought... Lachlan Cutlass did not say he wanted to take me on a date.

I sucked down a gulp of orange juice from a glass on the tray. "A date?" My pitch rose at the end like a schoolgirl going through puberty.

"You get some sleep tonight, rest up. If you're well enough, I'll take you out tomorrow night. You don't feel up to it, we can wait till the time is right, but I'm taking you on a date."

Oh holy Moses. He did say that. He said it a few times. My stomach plummeted, the itching stopped, and my heart pounded against my ribs.

"Like a little-sister, big-brother date?" I need him to verify exactly what the heck he was on about.

"No. A man and a woman date. The kind where I kiss you at the end." A rough rumble coated his words.

My mouth dropped open. Speak, brain, speak. "Kiss... me?"

He grinned and cute wrinkles appeared at the corners of his eyes. My heart melted. The sexiest man alive wanted to kiss me, and he was going about it in one of the nicest ways I could imagine. Lachlan had dominated all my fantasies for as long as I could remember. But they were only dreams. Never to come true. He seemed totally serious now. I had no idea what had gotten into him, but I knew his pattern. I knew he'd boss me around and leave again. So I knew how I had to respond.

"No." It didn't come out as firm as I would have liked but at least I'd said it.

"No?"

"We can't go on a date. Or kiss." My tone made it clear his idea was completely absurd. He was setting me up for some kind of fall, and I was old enough now to see through it.

"Why?"

"Because you're my brother's best friend!"

"I already discussed it with him."

"You did? And you're still alive?"

"He was surprised, but took it better than I expected."

I looked around all the corners of the room and on the ceiling. "Is there a video feed somewhere? Are you trying to get me in trouble with the DEA? Because you've already done that."

"I screwed up. Should've called off the bust when I saw you. Then you never would've had to go through all this with the withdrawals and the detox."

"Yes, but then I wouldn't have this experience. This is good. I don't have to be afraid anymore of having to shoot up. I know I can handle it, and I can get through it and not get addicted. I also have a lot more empathy for the people who get hooked cuz it's so easy. It's just such a slippery slope."

"It is incredibly easy."

"There's a boy, Jeremy. Slade sold him heroin. He was dealing to support his addiction. He looked like you. I felt just like my dad must have felt when he saw you. A life with such potential wasted. He's somebody's son or brother. He could've been someone that other people look up to, like you. He could grow up to be a Navy SEAL fighting for our country or a swim team captain. He could fall in love and be someone's everything, but all that he can't have until he gets out of where he is and makes a new start. I want to help him."

"I get it. I've seen it too. We can't help them all."

"I want to help Jeremy. My dad did it for you. It's my turn to pay it forward."

"You know where to find this Jeremy kid?"

"Yeah."

"Then we'll find him and help him."

"Thank you."

"Sleep now. We'll talk more about our date in the morning."

Oh my lord. Our date.

How could I sleep when a date with Lachlan Cutlass was on the table?

"I'll be on the couch if you need me."

I DID MANAGE TO SLEEP and felt better when I woke. I joined Lachlan at his kitchen table, where he'd prepared a plate of waffles with whipped cream and a cup of coffee for me. He'd already eaten his.

"Those look delicious."

"All for you."

"Yum." I sat down and tucked in.

"Take those vitamins too. Your body needs to replenish."

"Thank you."

He was quiet till I finished eating. "How're you feeling?"

"Better. Itchy skin gone, no pain. Just feel like I've been through a lawn-mower a few times."

"You up for our date tonight?"

"About the date. I did some thinking."

"Uh-oh. Nevada's been thinking. Anything could come out of her mouth now. And I bet I couldn't guess what it is. Alright. Tell me what you've been thinking."

"I won't date you."

He didn't blink or move. Finally, he said, "Colt will come around."

"It's not Colt. It's you."

"Me? What's wrong with me?"

"Nothing. That's the problem. You're perfect."

His head snapped back. "Explain."

"You're perfect. Captain of the swim team, flawless body, excellent grades, made the SEALs. Six years of service and you ease into a posi-tion at the Bureau with no injuries, no combat fatigue? They must be thrilled to have a Special Forces operator on their roster. I bet you're teaching their agents a few things. Have you ever slipped up?"

"Nev..."

"I'm the opposite of perfect. I blew my first undercover case by shooting up heroin. My tummy's too round, not firm and ripped like yours. My body is pretty much made out of wine and coffee. A baggage claim has less emotional issues than I do. I live in a bubble somewhere between reality and make believe. My finances are a mess. I could go on."

"No. No. I hear you." He looked down.

"It's fine if you want to torture yourself trying to attain perfection, but you expect me to be perfect too. I can't live up to that. Why do you think I kept my job at the DEA secret from you and Colt? Because it didn't fit your idea of what my life should be. You told me flat-out I wasn't suited for it, but I went and did it on my own with virtually no support from anyone in my family, not even emotional support. I'm sorry the op went longer than I expected, and you went crazy looking for me, but I had to do this. I'm an orphan. My parents are dead. I went to Quantico, I passed their tests, both physical and mental, and I got placed under Aquino with Slade. That assignment was my one chance to get to Greco, and you walked in and shut me down."

He looked up at me and his eyes were soft. "Are you done?"

"No. I'm not. Don't you see? The DEA wanted me. They graduated me. They knew all my flaws and accepted me, hired me, and trusted me in my role as an agent. A bureaucracy had more faith in me than my own family."

"You done now?" His voice was patient. How could he stay calm when my guts were being pulled from my body.

"Not yet. I've been holding this in a long time. So you want to take me on a date? Now? Do you know what I've been through with you? I spent all my life looking up to you, lusting after you, wanting you, letting you hold me when I fell, letting you touch me in ways that drove me wild wanting you, only to be told over and over again, he's your big brother, just looking out for you. And then I watched the most important person in my life," he reached out and put a hand on my calf, "Yes, over and over again I watched the most important person in my life walk away, get on a plane to do missions where he had a high chance of getting killed, and I had no claim to him, nothing to hold on to. So, you see why we can't go on a date? I can't put my imperfect self out there like that, only to be gutted when you leave for the next perfect part of your life."

I took a deep breath. He raised an eyebrow.

"Now I'm done."

"Come here." He opened his arms.

"No."

"Come sit your perfect ass down on my lap and let's get real."

He tugged my hand till I fell into his lap. My shoulder pressed into the plane of his chest, and the heat from his body instantly warmed me. He nailed me with that look again. "I'm not perfect. I guess I just didn't let you see my flaws."

At least he was admitting it. "You really didn't. Do you have any?"

He laughed. "I made it through BUD/S by the hair on my balls. I passed out in the pool. *Me*. The swimmer. I passed out in a fucking swimming pool."

"You did?"

"And those SEAL missions? They call me Lefty because I had a rep for mixing up coordinates. I sent my team the wrong way half the time. A team of six of the best military minds in our nation nearly died because of me."

"That's combat though. It's so unpredictable." Everyone gets coordinates mixed up at times, especially when lack of sleep takes over.

"This job? FBI Agent? I got made on my first assignment. The mark figured me out in two days."

"How?'

"My disguise wasn't good enough. My alias wasn't solid. The bad guys clued her in. FBI closed the case. I failed. Her name was Tessa. Let her down too cuz she trusted me, and I led her on. She was almost shot. Her husband, Rogan, had to get around me to save her. Kid name Zook Guthrie had the evidence all along. We didn't even need to send Tessa in. Costly error on my part."

"Is it wrong I feel good to hear that?"

"No."

"Other mistakes I made. Big ones. Trying to control your life, not telling you how I really felt, not sharing my failures. Worst of all, not telling you how everything you think is a flaw makes you warm, solid, unique, and incredibly sexy."

"Sexy?"

"Sexy as hell. Been driving me crazy for years."

"Oh."

"Yeah. Oh."

"So if you can forgive me, accept my flaws, say yes to a date, we can start moving toward who we're meant to be."

Who we're meant to be? We're meant to be... dating? "Yes." My reply came out breathy.

"Good. I have a perfect idea."

Oh there he goes with the perfect again. "I'll plan the date."

"Uh, no."

"I wanna see how imperfect you can be."

"Oh no. Now I'm worried."

"Don't be. Tonight after you get home from work?"

"Alright."

His hand slid up into my hair, wrapped around the base of my skull, and squeezed. "I'm gonna kiss you now. Then I'll stop because I got a meeting in Chelsea in thirty minutes. But this will be the last time I'm gonna stop without following through."

I swallowed the big lump in my throat. "Following through?"

"After this kiss, unless you tell me to stop, we're gonna keep kissing until you've had at least two orgasms and I've had my fill. Now, considering I waited this long, I can't imagine ever getting my fill."

"Oh."

"Oh yeah, you and I are gonna get to know each other's imperfections real good real fast."

"Okay."

Then he kissed me. Hard and soft at the same time. I closed my eyes and let him take over. And he did. Tasting me like a fine wine. My breath stuttered, a stirring in my belly flared up, making me want him more than I ever had. It was beautiful. I felt like I'd never been kissed before. And I hadn't, not like that. Not like I was precious and desirable and the center of his universe. And never by Lachlan. My brother's best friend. My high school crush. Kissing me.

I reached for him slowly, hesitant to break this trance, scared if I moved we'd return to who we were before. Friends—the overprotective big brother and the helpless little sister.

His tongue teased my lips and our tongues met. The euphoria of being high hit me again, exploding through my body as instantly as the drug had done.

My fingers scratched and grabbed his hair. God, he had thick, luscious hair. He tasted warm and sweet like the waffles. I wanted to crawl inside that kiss and stay forever. And I knew then, we could never go back to being just friends. We'd crossed the point of no return. This kiss toppled mountains and broke down walls. We'd never be the same again.

He pulled away slowly, licking his lips and piercing me with molten eyes under heavy lids. This was a side of Lachlan I'd never seen. A few times, when we were cuddling, I thought I felt an erection pressing against my leg, I thought I saw heat in his eyes, but I always told myself it was my imagination. Lachlan couldn't want me that way. But the way he looked now. I was wrong. He could certainly want me that way, and he did—right now.

He cleared his throat. "I have to go to work. Colt will be by. Slade is going to bring your coworkers from the DEA if you're ready to see your friends."

"I'm ready." Boy was I ready, not for the day, but for the night. Lachlan was going to take me on a date where he kissed me, and he wouldn't stop till I had at least two orgasms. Holy Man of La Mancha. I could not wait.

He grinned and traced his finger under my lips. "Bye, babe. I'm glad we talked about this."

Uh. "Me too." God, talking was hard.

He stepped away slowly, adjusting his slacks as he opened a drawer by the door. He strapped on a shoulder holster and checked his service weapon. Holy smokes, the man was hot. With a gun under his arm and that leather harness, he was deadly. "There's a dress you have. Sort of a forest green. Looks pretty with your eyes and hair."

Um, sorry. Was busy staring at your shirt as it pulled tight across your chest. A dress? I did like to wear deep greens to complement my hair.

"Cut low in front."

"I think I know the dress."

He turned back and gave me more of his fiery gaze. "You wear that one for me."

Oh there he goes bossing me around, expecting me to be perfect. "If I don't?" I smiled at him to challenge him.

"Anything you wear, I'll be stoked to be the one taking you out. That green dress though, spent years imagining taking it off you. It happens in reality, I could die happy."

My tummy flipped and flopped and fluttered. Holy sweet baby Jesus. Lachlan had joked about sex over the years, but I'd never seen this side of him. The few women I'd seen him with, there was nothing sexual in the way he talked to them or touched them.

This Lachlan was a walking, talking sex machine. It was like I knew a secret about the mysterious man no one else knew.

I might wear that green dress just to see more of sex-machine Lachlan.

Chapter 6

Lachlan

"Nevada Lacy. What the hell are we doing here?"

The fluorescent yellow sign of her Up With Yoga gym cut through the darkness of night in Somerville. She sat next to me in my truck, smelling good and looking sexy as hell in the forest-green dress I'd asked her to wear. She'd washed some of the brown out of her hair, hints of amber shining through again. Her skin glowed, that green shit she used worked like magic.

Another round of nerves zipped through my system. I'd gone out with Nev to parties and concerts, but tonight much more than fun balanced on the line. By the end of this date, I wanted her to understand how much I loved her, and I wanted her to accept she was mine. If I didn't succeed, I'd... No. Failure was not an option. Never surrender. My mantra.

If it didn't happen tonight, I'd regroup and try a different tactic tomorrow. If she made me wait, fine. But based on the kiss this morning and the fact she wore the dress, I had a feeling she wanted it as much as I did, and she'd been waiting for this as long as I had.

"I want to see you be imperfect. How does the infallible man handle a challenge?"

Infallible? Hardly. No one was bulletproof. But she'd picked a physical activity I could do in my sleep. "What makes you think I'll be challenged? Aerial stunts can't be too much harder than an obstacle course."

She laughed. "Oh, this is gonna be fun."

55

We walked inside Up With Yoga. Through the dim lights, all I saw was a big statue of Buddha on the counter, palm fronds painted on wooden walls, and her friend Crystal sitting in the reception area. Crystal was in her mid-30s, thick bangs that hung into her eyes and moved when she blinked. She smiled, popped up from her seat, and rushed to Nevada.

"Oh my god. I missed you so much."

"I missed you too, Crystal."

"How's Shanti?"

"Lachlan's been taking good care of him."

Her chin dipped and she gave me some flirty eyes. "Hello, Lachlan. Looking hot tonight."

I was wearing gray slacks and a burgundy button down shirt, dress shoes, and a black leather belt. Nothing special, but I thought it looked respectable for our first date.

Crystal handed Nevada a set of keys. "Let's do lunch to catch up, but tonight, the gym is yours. Be careful in there."

As she left, she called back, "Rub his belly."

I held my hands up, looking at Nevada. "Rub his belly."

"She meant Buddha, you nerd."

She rubbed the statue's belly and I followed her into the gym, checking her ass as it swayed. Those heels made her legs look like they never ended.

One light in the center illuminated a long silk fabric hanging from the ceiling. The sparkly teal green stood out as the only color in the otherwise muted room. I'd seen Nevada do aerial yoga at home in a hammock attached to her door jamb, but this one hung from a fifty-foot ceiling.

"Okay, Mr. Perfect. Show me what you can do." She stepped back.

"You just want me to climb it?"

"Yep. Just climb it."

"Piece of cake."

How hard could this be? I jumped up and grabbed on with both hands. My legs wrapped around nothing and the fabric slipped right out. I landed on my feet and stared at her.

"It's like tissue paper."

"Navy SEALs only climb thick strong ropes? What if you're in a situation where you need to climb silk curtains, for example?"

"In all my years with the Navy and the FBI, I've never had to climb a silk curtain."

"Let's say you're spying on a Russian diplomat. You must climb the silk curtains of the embassy to infiltrate."

A highly unlikely scenario, but okay.

On my next attempt, I made it up a few pulls. My feet couldn't get any traction. I either had to use arm strength all the way up or find a way to get my feet in there. I wrapped the silk around one leg and still couldn't get a hold. The fabric slipped right off my leg.

I let go and spun once as I fell on my ass, green silk keeping one foot up in the air. "How the hell do you do this?"

She laughed for a good long time. "The fabric is sticking to your clothes. Try taking them off."

"Oh really? Okay." I unbuttoned my shirt and enjoyed the way her eyes grew hot as she saw my abs.

"You got a new scar? Two of them?" Her fingertips passed over the shrapnel wounds on my chest.

"More than two. They patched me up fine." I turned, letting her see the scars on my back.

She gasped and skimmed her hand down them, leaving a trail of warmth behind. "I was always terrified for you. Checked the CIA database, always looking for injured or killed SEALs on the news, waiting to hear bad news."

I faced her again and pulled her into my arms. "I got lucky. Made it back to you." I glanced back to the silk hanging from the ceiling. "Pants too?"

"Mmm, yes. Can't do this in slacks."

The look in her eyes seemed genuine. This wasn't some prank to record this whole thing and post it on the DEA website.

"I've seen you in a Speedo many times."

"I'm not wearing a Speedo." I turned my back on her and undid my pants, giving her a slow reveal of my ass. I'd picked these coral boxer briefs to match her hair, which was darker tonight, but still, the color always reminded me of her. I turned and grinned at her.

She clicked her tongue as she took in the brand name, American Hero, across the waistband.

I wasn't embarrassed. Getting naked with Nev was goal number two of the night. I didn't think we'd get there this fast or this way, but you wouldn't hear me complaining.

Holding her close made me half-hard, so my package filled out the front enough to impress her more than what she'd ever seen in my Speedo.

I gave the silks another go and, sure enough, without my clothes, I was able to get a foothold I could work with. I climbed up about ten feet and looked down at her. "How's that?"

"Really, really nice."

She enjoyed watching my ass in my underwear struggle with this ridiculous excuse for a rope.

"Now do some tricks."

Tricks? I split the fabric into two pieces and tried to get my foot in there. It wouldn't stick. I wrapped it around my waist to hold me in place. I lost five feet. It wasn't graceful but I didn't fall. I struggled with that damn thing for ten minutes and couldn't get any tricks out. But at least I'd made her laugh, so I played it up for her.

I finally spun out of the tangled mess and hit the ground on my ass again.

"You find this entertaining?"

"Mmm-hmm."

"Your turn."

The smile on her lips turned tight, and she stepped back. "Oh no. This was all about you."

"We're not leaving this place till you show me how it's done."

She looked down at the floor and crossed her arms around her stomach. Not buying her shy act. I'd seen her do this in her apartment. Shy didn't last long on Nevada.

"I know you're out of practice, but getting back to your old routines might be good for you. I'd enjoy the hell out of it too."

She eyed the silks like they taunted her. Oh yeah, she wanted the challenge.

"You feeling up to it?"

"I feel great. I'm fine."

She actually did look healthy. A good night's sleep in her own sheets with her stuff around her did wonders for her recovery. "So take off your dress."

Her gaze rose to mine, her eyes twinkling. "I'm not taking off my dress."

"From what I hear, you can't do aerial yoga with clothes on. The silk will stick."

"That's so unfair."

"Hey, I'm standing here in my underwear."

Her face shifted, her lips twitching and she reached back for her zipper. I knew she'd go for it.

"Let me." As I helped her with it, a glossy silk bra came into view. I had to bite my lip when I saw the top of a white silk thong framing the freckled skin of her ass. Oh yes, this was so happening. Right here. Right now.

"My god, what you do to me, Nev."

"Huh?" She turned around, holding the dress over her front.

"Everything about you turns me on."

"Nuh uh."

She didn't believe me? I pulled her body against mine and closed my eyes. "Everything. Your lower lip when you smile, the curves of your hips, your voice, and your hair." I ran my palm over her wavy locks. "But mostly it's what's in here." I kissed just below the small of her neck. "You've got a rare heart, Nev. Traveled the world haven't met a soul as genuine and absolutely pure as yours."

She lowered her gaze. Might be hard for her to hear stuff like that from me, but she'd have to get used to it. She was getting it every day for the rest of her life.

I bent my head so we could meet at eye level. "I can be in a room full of women and not get turned on. But I can't be around you a second without lightning forking through my whole body. Everything about you is amplified. You're alive, you live in the moment, but you're also totally not in the moment, you're somewhere else at the same time."

"Wow."

"Yeah. Lots of wow. I'll tell you more later. Now go up there. Show me your beauty."

She dropped the front of the dress, and my dick became fully hard. I watched her thong-covered ass as she walked over to an entertainment center and fiddled with the buttons. After a short while, a mournful electric guitar riff filled the room.

"This your song?" I asked her.

She didn't make eye contact with me as she strode back to the hammock. "No, it's yours."

Mine?

She hopped up on the silk, lifted her lower half and twisted her legs in the bands all in one practiced motion. Hanging upside down, her hair flowed below her like an extension of her body.

Her legs split open and with seemingly no effort, she started to spin. She struggled with the scarves as she tried to return to an upright position, growling in frustration.

"You're doing great. Don't worry."

The deep concentration lines on her face relaxed, and her movements became seamless. With her eyes closed, she transitioned through the yoga poses like she hadn't been away eight months.

The singer sang about a man who hadn't been there for a woman. God, it *was* my song. And it was incredibly depressing. My song made her turn inward and feel like she wasn't good enough. That would change right now. I wouldn't make her sad ever again.

I moved closer, looking up to see her directly above me.

"Twirl me."

I grabbed the silk and tugged her counterclockwise. She arched back to increase the centripetal force, and she smiled for the first time since she'd climbed up.

The man in the song begged for a chance to try to be good enough and here I was, standing at her feet, pleading. Or maybe the song wasn't about me at all. Maybe she longed to give herself a chance, talking to her own thoughts holding her back from achieving what she wanted. We'd have plenty of time to get to the center of that.

Hanging by one foot, she slid down so her face was upside down, level with mine. I tried to kiss her smiling lips, but the sway prevented us from connecting. I had to use the slack fabric to stop her and plant one on her. She kissed me back, but before I could deepen it, she pulled herself up and spiraled to the ceiling, wrapping the silk around her midriff as she scaled higher. She looked angelic, the white bra and the turquoise scarf framing her breasts and ass. Beyond this world.

"Catch me." She released and dropped all the way down with her arms over her head, spinning like a horizontal ballerina.

I reacted just in time to catch her in my arms.

She fell with abandon, totally trusting me to catch her. The song ended, only our breaths whispering through the empty gym.

Chapter 7

———

S he wrapped her arms around my neck, and I carried her to the mat. "You're phenomenal. I can't believe how gorgeous you looked up there."

"I play that song when I'm missing you. The singer's last name is Lachlan."

I pressed my lips to her temple, kissed her sweet lips, and ran my nose down her neck, taking in her warmth and sweet lavender scent. "I'm sorry I disappointed you and made you doubt yourself. I..." We should talk. Not kiss. Talk this through so she knows where I'm at. But damn her skin felt soft on my lips and a fifteen-year-old ache in my balls was making decisions for me.

"It's okay." Her head dropped back, giving me better access to the length of her neck. Green light. The go signal I'd been waiting for. But...

"I fucked up. I held back. I should've trusted you. We could've been together all this time."

She opened her eyes and placed her warm palm on my cheek. "Shoulds and coulds will drive you crazy. We ran different courses, but all paths led us back here."

"There's more we need to talk about."

"Can it wait till later? Because I'm about to make you keep your promise."

"Which one?"

"The one where you kiss me through at least two orgasms."

A groan escaped from deep in my throat. "God, you're killing me."

She kissed me, wet and sweet and deep. I lowered her head and lay down on top of her. My dick definitely wanted to pound her into the mat. But the reason I'd waited still existed. Nothing changed with this kiss. I still owed her the truth.

"The reason I waited was not because you were not good enough."

"Mmm?"

"I waited because I'm a recovering addict."

Her mouth dropped open, her eyes wide. "I never saw you do drugs."

"I haven't used since the end of my freshman year at Boston College."

"And why did this keep us apart? Why are we talking about it now when there are much more important issues at hand?" She palmed my hard cock through my underwear.

I had to focus on a spot on the wall to keep my thoughts straight. Why did I need to talk about this now? Oh yeah. "I had a weakness. One that killed your parents, and I knew you'd never accept me if you knew. You'd never believe I'd be strong enough to stay clean."

"But you didn't ask me?"

"No. You had a boyfriend. I joined the Navy to punish myself. During every challenge, I swore I wouldn't come back to you until I had mastered the discipline to be the man you need."

"You flogged yourself for this all this time? Why? It was so unnecessary. I would've left any boyfriend for you. I'd take you any way you came. Addict or not."

"Really? You wouldn't be worried your drug-addict boyfriend was using? Every time I didn't call, every time I came home stressed out, you wouldn't worry about me getting hooked up with Greco and getting killed like your parents?"

Her brow furrowed and she sat up, propping her elbows behind her. "You made a lot of assumptions about what I would think. You never gave me a chance to answer."

"Now's the time, before we make love, because after this there's no turning back. I'm still an addict. I still feel the urge, but I'm solid. I know I'll never go back."

She grabbed my face and pulled me down on top of her, our lips a centimeter apart. "I believe you." I felt her smile against my lips. "But you could've told me this earlier... or later."

I kissed her softly. "Shoulds and coulds will drive you crazy."

A frustrated grunt accompanied her widening smile. "Your conscience clean now? Can we proceed to the exchange of fluids? Because you've been hiding a lethal weapon in your Speedo all these years, and I want to get my mouth on it, if you wouldn't mind scheduling that into your agenda for tonight."

Once again Nev reminded me why I loved her. I could always trust her to say it like it is. She accepted my flaws without question and basically told me to let it go. I could do that.

I found the clasp of her bra and snapped it open. Slowly, I lowered it, revealing her sumptuous breasts. I kissed the scar on her shoulder before sucking in one rosy pink nipple, teasing it to a peak. Then the other.

Her hands skimmed over my shoulders and squeezed my biceps. "God, I can't believe this is happening."

I stopped and caught her hooded gaze. "No one else, Nev."

"I didn't think you liked me that way."

"I love you that way." How could she not know?

"You..."

"I love you that way and this way and all ways."

"Oh my god."

"It's true. Gonna show you now."

I started slowly, exploring her inch by inch, curve by curve. Her hands roamed my back, her nails scratching trails up and down. The first touch of her body this way had me hard as hell, wanting to rush it, and take it slow too. Soon, we were both naked, our bodies rubbing together, and I couldn't hold back anymore. I'd explode if I didn't get inside her.

I kissed down her navel and tasted her sweet pussy. Heaven. She moaned and arched her back. I didn't hold back, wanting her to come fast and hard. And she did. She groaned and pulsed on my lips, riding it out with her eyes closed, her head back. The noises coming from her drove me crazy. I had to leave her to snag a condom from my pants.

"No condoms." She spoke quickly, panting.

"What?"

"The Bureau tests you. DEA tests me. I'm on the Pill. No condom necessary."

Yes, this woman was made for me. I returned to her, lined our bodies up, and kissed her. When I finally slid inside Nev, I'd found where I belonged. My lost soul had a home.

I'd never connected like this with anyone. She felt it too by the way she responded, reached for me, pulled me closer. It wasn't perfect on the floor of the gym. The mat squeaked, and it couldn't have felt good on her bare skin, but it was us. Finally.

Her whimper signaled she'd found it. I pumped inside her, kissing her through a second orgasm. God, she was beautiful when she came, moaning loudly like she didn't care if anyone heard.

I slammed into her hard, burying all the pain and lost time in her. It rose up in my balls, strong like the pull of gravity when a helo takes off. Everything about her gripped me tight, pulled me in, and made it safe to let go. So I jumped out the door and fell into freefall. Total freedom, total release, totally shattered. We came together, both of us grunting and panting through the overwhelming force of it.

After endless moments, we landed, back on the gym floor, safe and sound. I planted my head in her shoulder and inhaled her scent. Lavender mixed with sage and sweat. "You're mine now. Body and soul. No one else. You and me.

"Yes, Lachlan." Her closed eyes fluttered open.

She was so receptive to my touch, my love, I wanted to stay here forever, breathing the same air, celebrating the barriers we broke through and looking forward to our future, but...

"Now I'll take you on our real date."

"This wasn't our real date?"

"This was incredible, and if I didn't have tickets to Cirque du Soleil, we'd be going at it again right now." Her eyes grew wide, and her guttural laugh looked sexy as hell on her. I could shove my dick in her open mouth and... uh... "But I do have tickets, so I'll show you some more of my imperfections at home after the show. In my bed."

"Oh my god."

"And in my shower. Maybe the kitchen counter." Yes, some whipped cream on her tits. Lots of ideas flooded my mind.

I kissed her again, but pulled away. I helped her clean up and dress. Turning off the lights and locking the gym, I said, "I hope we didn't leave any evidence behind."

"If we did, Crystal will be thrilled for me. She loves you." Nevada gave me a sexy just-fucked smile, her hair a tousled mess. God, I loved seeing her this way, a sensuous woman, enjoying her body, celebrating life.

"How could she not? I'm perfect, remember?" I took her hand in mine.

She smacked my chest. "Shut up. You looked like a drunk monkey on the silks."

"True. Oh man." I stopped in my tracks, pulling her to a stop too.

"What?"

"Wanted to fuck you in the hammock, your legs spread in the splits."

"Mmm. I wanted to suck your dick."

"You did?" Yes, I love this woman.

"What time does the show start?" She checked her watch as I checked mine.

"An hour."

She looked over her shoulder at the closed door to the gym. "And if we're a little late?"

"Wouldn't bother me."

My cock swelled again as I guided her back into the gym. We didn't waste time getting hot and heavy fast. We made love again. This time with her upside down in the hammock, her beautiful hair brushing the floor, her arms above her head, hanging loose. She slipped and slid around. I fumbled through it. We both came hard, laughing and loving every second. It was perfect.

Chapter 8

A girl shouldn't have to track her own partner. She should be able to trust him to keep her in the loop if anything went down. Unless there'd been a breach in trust. For example, say the girl shot heroin for the case and almost overdosed, or the girl harbored a vicious vendetta against a Mafia capo, the partner might think he had a good reason to leave her out of the action. He'd be wrong. Partners should confide in each other above all else, even the DEA. The bond should run deeper than the agency.

So when Slade gave me a weak excuse for missing a meeting at the office, I followed him. Trailing him with a rental car and a tracking device felt dirty and disloyal. But in the end, a girl had to protect herself by staying in the know.

The tracking signal led me to the FBI holding facility housing Darin Aquino. My heart jumped into my throat when Slade, dressed in his slick suit with his hair spiked up like his Johnny Blanco alias, emerged from Johnny's car and walked—with Johnny's limp— through the front entrance.

Twenty minutes later, he got back in his car and pulled away. I tracked him through a heat run we used to do when we were on the Aquino case. We'd make turns and switchbacks used to lose any possible tails. He parked at the hideout we'd lived in together. A place he wouldn't go to dressed as Johnny unless the case had been reactivated.

Shaking my hair out, I checked my look in my rearview mirror. I added some eyeliner, took off my work shirt, leaving me in only a white tank top and jeans, and walked barefoot up to the apartment.

Quick-quick-slow-slow. Our secret knock.

Slade opened the door and gave me a *you shouldn't be here* look.

I brushed past him into the place. "Johnny." Inside, the old carpet and single beds brought all the memories back. Living here with Johnny, working at the strip joint, missing Shanti and my family so much it hurt. Then the hardest part, selling drugs to poor kids like Jeremy. "You clear this place?"

He sat in front of his laptop at the folding table in the center of the room. "Yes. Listen, Nev..."

"No, you listen. Don't shut me out. I don't care what orders you were given. I'm on this case, and until I'm officially removed, you include me in everything."

"Agent Seneco wants you out."

"Then tell him to remove me." Seneco wouldn't do it because it would raise too many questions about the case at trial.

"I agree with him. Let me do this."

"I know you met with Aquino just now. Why?"

He sighed and looked away. "He wants me to meet with Gunderson, maintain his flow of goods while he's locked up. Thinks he's getting out of the charges."

God, I hated being excluded from things like this. "I'm in."

"Not a good idea, Nev."

I slammed my palm onto the wobbly table. "I'm in."

He looked up at me, his eyes worried for me. "Could be a set up."

Men had looked at me that way all my life. Worried. "Don't care." Gunderson would lead us straight to Greco. Let me take my own risks.

He squinted as he looked at the window he couldn't see through. Even if the curtain wasn't there, all he would see would be the brick walls of the alley. "Lachlan will kick my ass if you got even a scratch."

Oh, please. Not Lachlan holding me back again. "Let me be in charge of me, okay? I can handle this. Don't tell me I can't."

"One condition. We go in for Gunderson and get out. No extensions for Greco."

Slade knew me too well. "Not giving up on Greco until he's dead."

He shook his head. "Better to dismantle him one soldier at a time."

"I want to dismantle his heart."

"One step at a time."

"Okay." I couldn't stand to be away from Lachlan that long anyway.

I sat down across from him. "Fill me in on the details."

HOURS LATER, WHEN I got home, Shanti rushed me. I bent down to receive his welcome-home kisses and give a good rub on his rump in the spot that makes him dance.

I was laughing when Lachlan came out of the kitchen, smiling, and wearing jeans.

Just jeans.

No shirt. No shoes. Just Lachlan's drool-worthy body and a pair of old faded jeans, the top button hanging open. He sauntered toward me with his arms coming out to embrace me.

Oh my Aunt Thelma, pick my jaw up off the floor, the man was stunning. He must've showered after work because his hair shined and curled a little like it did when it was wet. He looked like a merman forced onto land, wearing jeans because he had to, but would be more comfortable in the water without them.

He invaded my personal space and pressed his lean body against me. We lined up so my eyes hit his Adam's apple, which was scruffy because apparently he didn't shave when he showered. My mouth hit the taut muscle of his shoulder, and I couldn't help but sink my teeth in just a little bit.

He rubbed up and down my back, his deep voice and heated breath kissing my ear. "How're you, babe?"

Turned on. Totally turned on. That's how I was. I smiled up at him. He groaned and kissed me. A warm, hot, wet welcome-home kiss, much better than Shanti's.

"When you're gone, I'm thinking about when you're gonna be home. When you get home, all I can think about is getting your clothes off and fucking you stupid. When I'm done fucking you, I'm planning the next time."

I felt the same way. "Me too."

He caressed my head, smoothing my hair down. His eyes lingered on my hair in his hands. "Glad the red is back."

"Yeah."

"I saved dinner for you. You didn't show, so Shanti and I ate together. Like the old days. Much prefer seeing your appetizing face at the table." I watched his ass in his jeans as he walked to the kitchen.

Taking a deep breath to calm my raging hormones, I set my purse and coat on the entry table. I disarmed my weapon and stashed it in the safe Lachlan had given me. In the kitchen, he showed me a refrigerated plate of grilled vegetables, long-life noodles, and teriyaki tofu. "You ate tofu?"

"Fuck no. I had a steak. Cooked your tofu with it." He popped the plate in the microwave. "Why were you late?"

He leaned against the counter and crossed his arms over his chest. I really wanted to lick my favorite spot between his pecs where he had a little patch of chest hair.

"Hmm?" he prompted me.

"Oh, uh. Working on some details with Slade." A trickle of excitement bubbled up my throat. We had a solid plan to take down Gunderson. After all the work Slade and I put in on this case, I could not wait to get an arrest.

His eye twitched. "You got a new case?"

"Old one, revived." I smiled at him. "Starts tomorrow."

"Which old one?"

Oh, right. I'd momentarily forgotten Lachlan's stance on this. "Aquino."

The heat in his eyes changed to stone. "He's locked up."

"He wants Johnny and me to keep his cash flow moving. Thinks he can get out of the charges." Shoot. I'd been working the desk with Slade since the last op. This was the first test of Lachlan's promise to accept me as I am.

The microwave beeped. My meal was ready, but he didn't move. His jaw set and mashed. "No."

"No what?"

"You are not doing this."

So much for his promise. "I am. It's my op. I want in on it."

Suddenly, I was facing one pissed-off Navy SEAL. Sex machine Lachlan had left the building. "You're throwing yourself at their feet."

"You have no faith in me at all? I can wear a prosthetic. I can wear a vest."

"You can't prepare for all scenarios. What if they force you to use again? You're gonna risk getting addicted to heroin?"

"Slade and I will be prepared." That should be good enough for him if he trusted me like he said he did.

"Slade's game is weak. He looked clean then pretended to shoot up and forgot to act high. He blew it."

"Aquino trusts Slade. He worked hard to gain that, and we can't throw it all away because you think it's too risky."

"I saw you kiss him."

Ugh. This fight was going there? Jealousy? After a month where we'd been together every free moment, as many of those in bed as possible. "For a job."

"Lines blur." He narrowed his eyes at me.

"How do you know?"

He drew back. Oh yeah, I hit a nerve. "Many agents have fallen for a mark or another agent. Not just me."

"You fell for a mark? Who?"

He looked away. "I didn't fall for her. The lines blurred is all I'm saying. It clouds your judgement. Are you doing this out of loyalty to Slade?"

"No. I'm doing this because it's my job, and I fought hard to get this position. This is why I didn't tell you or Colt about it. I knew you would react this way and try to stop me." I sighed. This sucked. He was betraying all the promises he made me. "I don't want to go in there without your support."

"Then don't go in because I won't support it."

"We could get Greco too."

The veins in his neck got tight and his muscles tensed. "That's insane. You are not going to bring down the Italian Mafia." God, angry Lachlan with no shirt on was hot as all get out.

I'd promised Slade I wouldn't go after Greco, but Lachlan was pissing me off so I wasn't going to give him that. "Who says I can't?"

He rushed me then, forcing the air from my lungs as he slammed me up against the wall. "I don't know whether to fuck you or fight you."

"Do both. Take it out on me."

His nostrils flared. "Damn, Nev."

I felt his erection dig into my hip, and my body responded instantly. Lachlan turned me on so fast, just his breath on my neck was enough to get me going, his whole body surrounding me, I didn't stand a chance.

He scooped me up, carried me to the bed, dropped me down, and I bounced a few times. He was on me in a second and loosening his pants at the same time.

I ripped off my shirt and bra. He worked down my bottoms. We'd never gotten naked quicker. He pushed my arms over my head and held my hands with one of his, the pressure from his wrist hurt, but not enough to complain. No, I liked his roughness. He treated me like I could handle it. And I could.

His free hand tickled my skin as it skimmed over the curves of my breast, across my navel, and between my legs to my center. My back arched into his touch.

"I gotta be there for you." His voice scratched like metal on granite. "All my life, I protected you. Now I'm supposed to let you go? I just got you."

He kissed down my neck, still holding my hands over my head, caressing my clit at the same time.

I could barely speak. "You need to let me do this."

"No."

Before I knew it, he flipped me over and tugged my hips up. His hand pressed my hands to the bed again. A whoosh of air hit my ears and a sting landed on my left ass cheek.

I peered up at him over my shoulder. His face burned red with his concentration. "Oh my god, Lachlan. Are you spanking me?"

He switched his hold on my wrists, and another smack came down on my right cheek. "Hell yes."

My whole body tensed, ready to fight, but as he did it again, the burn tingled, and my body wanted it, bad. So I raised my hips and lowered my shoulders, waiting for the next touch of his palm.

His breathing was heavy, and with each smack, my skin heated, my core ached for him. He stopped to rub his hand over my sex, get it wet, and then spank me again and again. I was surprised I liked it, but we needed this right now.

"Mine." He lined up and worked his cock in.

"Yes, god."

His groin slapped my heated ass, his balls swinging forward, his abs against my back. His fingers pinched my nipple hard and rolled, sending sparks all over my body. I loved it. He was totally dominating me. Staking his claim. Every cell in my body sang for him.

He released my wrists and worked my clit. We both grunted as we found resonance, moving as one at the same speed in the same wavelength. He was hot and wet and sticky and it hurt but it also felt fantastic.

My orgasm pushed through me like a tidal wave. I came hard, crashing all around him. "God, Lachlan."

"One more time."

He worked my sensitive clit again until I moaned through a second one. Then he took his fill, pumping into me with all the power of a tank. He planted himself deep and groaned.

His lips pressed to my neck as he came inside me. We crashed to the bed. His mouth kissed along my cheek to my lips. I could stay in this kiss forever.

We lay there for precious minutes before he pulled out and stood. "Be right back."

I felt the loss of him as I watched him walk naked to the bathroom. He came back with a warm washcloth. He cleaned me up gently and lovingly. I turned around and he laid on top of me and kissed me.

"I wasn't there."

"What? Where?"

"The night your mom was murdered. I wasn't there." He sounded agonized.

"This isn't the same as my mom's murder."

"It's not? It's not you telling me to go to a swim meet after you'd already suffered all day through your dad's funeral? It's not you telling me to leave you alone when everything in me wanted to stay with you?"

"No."

"How's it different? Tell me how this is not going to end with me getting a phone call that you got shot."

"I'll have my team this time."

"Your team is just as human as I am. They make mistakes."

"I made you go. It's not your fault. You could've been killed too."

"I could've saved her." He said it like he'd been repeating it in his head for the last fifteen years.

"No, don't think that."

His eyes looked over my head. "I don't want to lose you now." His voice was weaker than I'd ever heard it.

"You won't."

"Don't take the op." His pleading broke my heart.

I looked away. "I'll be careful."

"Fuck." His forehead fell into my neck. "Fuck!"

"I'm sorry I'm not who you want me to be." I wasn't the girl who would follow his orders, no matter how much sense he was making.

"That's not it." His eyes focused on me, his voice deep and intense. "You are everything I want you to be, and I'm proud as fuck you're brave enough to do this, but... I can't watch."

"Watch what?"

"If you're going under with Slade, I can't watch. You be careful in there. I'll come back to you when it's over."

Come back to me? He was leaving? "Where are you going?"

"Not far."

Why did I not believe him? Why did I feel like he'd be very far away?

"You promise you won't interfere?"

He closed his eyes. I'd hurt him, but he needed to accept this about me. "You won't see me."

"I'll miss you."

"Yeah."

He kissed me. "I love you, Nevada Lacy."

"I love you too, Lachlan Cutlass."

He rose from the bed and moved to his closet. I wanted to cry or scream or something to fix this. But what could I do? He wasn't telling me no, so there was no fight. He was simply saying he couldn't watch. I understood because I'd worried about him every time he left on a mission. Now the tables had turned.

"Don't need these anymore." He slapped an envelope on the nightstand, kissed me one more time, and left the room.

Oh gosh. Oh no.

The front door slammed shut.

On the nightstand, he left two Cirque du Soleil tickets.

And two first-class boarding passes to Las Vegas.

For this weekend.

Chapter 9

"One, two, three." Slade checked the audio transmitter in his watch. Agent Teo Vargas, the DEA communications specialist, recorded Slade's voice on a laptop and gave him a thumbs up.

Ten of us crammed into the small command center on a fishing boat moored at Dock 9 in Boston Harbor, two slips south of Gunderson's yacht. The logistics of the harbor presented a slight challenge, but nothing our team couldn't handle.

Agent Miranda Dunn handed me an aged-leather heroin kit. "Syringe in here's loaded with a dose of Amytal large enough to bring a full-sized man to complete narcosis in less than fifteen seconds, if you get a vein. Sub-Q might take thirty seconds or more depending on size and tolerance. Most likely not lethal, assuming no other narcotics in the system at the time."

"What if it's mixed with heroin?" I opened the kit to get a look at the syringes. One full, two empty.

"Don't mix it with heroin," Agent Dunn said, matter-of-factly.

"What if we have no choice?" Anything could happen during an operation like this.

"Risk of death by overdose increases exponentially when combined with other narcotics." She raised her eyebrows and waited for that to sink in.

"Right." So we had potentially lethal doses in play.

The syringe required closer proximity than a gun, but Gunderson required us to be unarmed for this meet, so the syringe would have to suffice.

Slade inspected the prosthetic on my elbow as the makeup artist finished the final touches on my track marks and bruises. "Looks good." I also had a thin armor plate under my hoodie. I'd colored my hair temporary brown again.

The last two weeks without Lachlan frazzled my nerves. The familiar bitter regret of him leaving with no definite return date had me constantly analyzing all the possible outcomes. My heart and body longed for his touch. Moving in with Slade made it all so much worse.

Lachlan left so much up in the air between us. Even though he'd asked me to come back to him at the end, the distance between us still felt final. Like he'd never forgive me for accepting this assignment with Slade.

My worries about Lachlan had to take a back seat because I needed my head in the game for today's meet.

Looking out the porthole, large bubbles erupted on the surface. Too big to be a fish, too small to be a vessel. "Did you guys check the water?"

"Of course." Agent Seneco peered out of an adjacent porthole. "It's clear. We have ten agents on the docks and five in the harbor."

"Good."

He showed me a live surveillance shot of the boat. "Gunderson has one crew member on the vessel with him. Teo ID'd him as Marco Vanetti, one of Greco's soldiers. He's waiting in the captain's bridge. Gunderson is in the cabin right now. No one else on the docks or the pier that we can see. Exit this dock, go wide north, and circle back, approach from the south."

My heart pounded and fear dropped in my tummy like a dead weight. I'd trained for this. I knew what to do, but still felt horribly underqualified.

Slade and I made it out to the yacht, walking casually even though inside we were both nervous as hell. As we climbed the ramp up, Gunderson came out and offered us a pleasant smile. Dressed in black slacks and a grey sweater, nothing about him said bad guy. Deceptively attractive.

"Hey, I hope you don't mind I brought my girlfriend." Slade helped me up onto the boat.

Gunderson took my hand as I stepped down. "Of course. She's lovely. Come. Sit. Drink."

We followed him to the outdoor dining area near the stern of the boat. He poured a dark liquid into three glasses on a rectangular table as we took seats, Slade to my left, Gunderson opposite me.

The yacht's engines rumbled beneath us. I shared a glance with Slade. We'd hoped to stay in port and make this quick. If we were going out into the harbor, my team would be farther away.

Gunderson focused his attention on me as we motored away from the dock. His eyes scrutinized my hair as he rubbed his chin with his fingers. Warning signals flared in my head. "You look familiar. What's your name, sweetheart?

I swallowed the lump in my throat and answered in the meek tone my alias used. "Nev."

"Mmm. Nev. I knew a girl named Nevada once." Oh shit. "Shame she died."

He recognized me. "That's too bad. Sorry to hear that."

"Yeah, so where's the stash? We're not here to talk about dead girls." His eyes flicked to Slade, disregarded him, and turned back to me.

He held up his phone, pointing it at my face.

Slade's energy hit me from the side. This was not good. Red flag. Red flag.

Gunderson tapped on his phone, concentrating hard. He looked up and his eyes saw right through me. "I thought I recognized you. Nevada Lacy. Frank Lacy's daughter."

No. No. No.

"I- What are you talking about?"

"Hey, hey, man. She's just my girl. You don't know her. Let's focus on the reason we're here." Slade tried to deflect him.

The wind and the waves blasted in my ears, but the silence screamed at me to run.

Gunderson licked his lips, and his eyes turned deadly. "I could swear I shot you that night."

I could swear I shot you that night.

A phantom pain pierced my shoulder. This couldn't be happening.

"Uh, no. Not me. Never been shot."

He sipped his drink. "How long has it been? Fifteen years? You grew up to be beautiful. Unfortunately, also a crack whore, but very pretty."

Slade pulled out his heroin rig and smacked it on the table. "C'mon, man. Stop the bullshit. Bring out the goods and let's test it." He left it pushed off to the side, closer to me, offering me a weapon.

"No, no. I'm more interested in this deal. What should we do with sweet Nevada who didn't die? A girl like her is worth a lot of money on the market. But then again, she's old and strung out. Maybe I'll finish the job now."

"Look. She isn't who you think she is, so just drop it."

"No. She's a liability. You see I got where I am today by killing her. My boss finds out I didn't finish the job, he'll have my head for dinner."

As we passed beyond the entrance to the harbor, the yacht slowed. The engines sputtered and we stalled, drifting off-course in Massachusetts bay.

Gunderson looked up to the captain's bridge. "What's wrong, Marco?"

"Engines died."

Gunderson stood and stepped closer to Marco. "Fix it. Fast."

"Yes, sir."

Slade's eyes scanned the water and saw the same thing I did, the Boston skyline getting smaller, a few pleasure craft and duck boats, but nothing like the boat our team used. Were they not able to leave the harbor with us?

Slade narrowed his eyes at me and tilted his head toward Marco. He peered up at Gunderson, looking ready to leap while he was distracted by the engines going out.

Slade leaped from his chair and tackled Gunderson. They hit the deck with a thud. Gunderson grunted as Slade landed two vicious punches to his face. Blood dripped from his nose as they wrestled on the floor.

Slade looked like he had the advantage, so I unwrapped the kit and grabbed the syringe. I tossed the cap and gripped it like a dagger. I needed to get to Marco before he reacted and pulled a weapon.

I took two steps away from the fight and toward the bridge. Marco had moved to the side of the bridge and he had his gun aimed at the two men wrestling on the deck.

"Johnny!"

Slade looked back just as Marco pulled the trigger. Slade took a bullet in his leg and Gunderson pushed him off. "Goddamn, Marco. You nearly hit me."

"Sorry, boss." Marco turned his gun at me. "What do you want me to do with her?"

"Shoot the bitch."

I dropped to my hands and knees and crawled to the side of the boat, where Marco couldn't reach me. He'd just have to take a few steps down, and he could shoot my brains out.

Gunderson pulled a weapon and followed me. "No, wait. I'll do it. It was my error. I'll correct it."

This was it. I was going to die on a boat in the bay. I'd never see Lachlan or Colt again. I didn't get to say goodbye. This would ruin Lachlan. He'd never recover from the guilt.

I heard Slade yell "No!"

Another shot echoed on the waves. I flinched and ducked my head.

A body hit the deck. But it wasn't mine.

Marco's body fell to the deck beside me, blood spreading through his shirt.

Oh my god! Who shot Marco? Did my team make it to us in time?

Gunderson turned to see where the shot came from. There. Off the stern. A man in black dive gear, aiming a rifle at Gunderson.

His face was covered, but oh my god, with those broad shoulders, he could be Lachlan. My heart leaped, telling me yes, it was him. He'd followed me. All the way out here.

Lachlan and Gunderson fired at each other. I couldn't track all the shots. All I could do was stay low and pray Lachlan had good aim. With all that gear though, and the rocking of the boat, getting a decent shot seemed impossible. Gunderson had the benefit of some cover on the boat, but Lachlan's position at the stern left him fully vulnerable.

Lachlan flinched, dropped his weapon, and fell backward into the water.

Gunderson ran to the stern of the boat and shot at the water.

No way was the man who murdered my mother going to shoot Lachlan too. He'd never take anything from me again.

I charged him from behind, holding back the tribal yell in my throat to keep some element of surprise. The needle made satisfying contact as it pierced his skin. The plunger went down fast and easy, despite my shaking hands. I left the needle in his neck and fell to my butt, scooting backward as he turned to see what happened. I'd hit him off-center, closer to his shoulder than his neck. Not ideal, but the Amytal was in his body. Please let it be deep enough.

Gunderson took two steps. C'mon, Amytal. C'mon work for me. Please. His arms and gun flailed like he wanted to shoot me, but he didn't have the motor control. His mouth dropped open, and a hideous groan came out. I glanced at Lachlan's rifle, about three feet out of reach. After one more heavy step toward me, he fell. The vibration of his body shook the deck like an earthquake. I scrambled to Lachlan's rifle, picked it up, and aimed it at him, finger on the trigger.

He rolled to his back. Technically, he didn't pose a threat any longer. I had no cause to kill him.

"DEA. Stay back." The tag team didn't have a visual on me. They wouldn't know he wasn't still attacking me. "Stay back," I yelled with false urgency. This man would not have the luxury of a trial and rotting in prison. Tyler Gunderson would meet his maker today.

I pulled the trigger. The first shot pierced his chest. That one was for my dad. The second shot hit his forehead. That one was for my mom. Goodbye, asshole.

The two seconds it took for his life to bleed out of him were the only seconds I could give him. Slade and Lachlan needed me.

"Man down! Man overboard. Clear. Clear. I need medics here stat."

When I made it to Slade, I found him awake, holding his leg and rocking.

"GSW to the leg. We need a tourniquet." I ripped off my hoodie and started to twist it into a rope.

Before he could answer, the tag team's boat pulled up beside us, a bunch of armed agents waiting to jump on board.

"The team is here. They'll help you. I need to check on Lachlan."

I ran to the side of the boat, stepped up, and jumped feet first. Ice-cold water soaked my clothes and gushed around me. The three seconds it took to surface felt like an hour. Don't let him be dead. Don't let Lachlan be dead.

"Lachlan!" I called out but my voice felt tiny in the waves and the wind. Where did he go?

His head surfaced about twenty feet away from me. I swam with all my might over to him. He was the swimmer, but I probably broke a few freestyle swim records to get to him.

"Are you okay?"

"He got me."

"Where? I need to get you on the boat. Oh god, Lachlan. Where are you shot?"

A glossy tint of red blood floated up to the surface on his left side.

"Shoulder."

The sound of a speedboat and the wake of waves hit us. I caught a glimpse of what looked like Tavian as he dove into the water. He surfaced next to Lachlan and wrapped an arm around his neck. He towed him back to his speedboat. "I got you."

I swam behind them. The cold finally hit me. My lips quivered, and I shook from head to toe.

Tavian must've been incredibly strong because he pulled Lachlan up over the side of the speedboat. I clung to the edge, trying to catch my breath. Lachlan, lying on the floor of the boat, removed his mask and looked at me. God, it was good to see his face. "Get her out."

"Let's check your wound first." Tavian cut a hole into Lachlan's wetsuit.

"Get her out of the goddamn water."

A gush of air burst from my lips. Shouting commands was a good sign he'd survive.

Tavian shook his head, came to the side of the boat, and gave me a hand. My knees banged on the side as he pulled my dripping wet body on board.

Tavian went back to work on Lachlan's wound as the DEA team pulled up beside us and jumped from their boat to ours. Teo took the wheel, started up the engine, and we headed back to shore.

———————

AT MASS GEN, DR. DARBY's hug reminded me of my mom. She always gave hugs that felt like hot cocoa after a day building snowmen.

"I'm glad everyone is okay. I'll check in with you tomorrow."

On her way out, she waved to Lachlan and Slade in their adjacent hospital beds. Colt sat quietly next to Slade's bed.

Lachlan was shirtless, a big gauze bandage over his left shoulder.

"I'd do it again," Lachlan said as his thumb caressed my hand.

I bent and pressed my lips to his forehead. "You'd better not."

He angled his head and I gave him a lip touch. "I fucked up." He looked down at our joined hands. "Couldn't find the dock, didn't have the right tools, and by the time I drained the fuel, it was too late. You guys had taken off into the harbor, so I just swam behind you."

"As usual, you went way overboard. But this time you were right. Saved me and Slade."

He touched his bandage and grinned. "We'll have matching scars."

"Yep. Inside and out."

"Yeah."

Chapter 10

———

Nevada

The lights in the arena dimmed. I grabbed Lachlan's hand and gave it a squeeze.

He smiled at me and kissed me. "Be right back."

"Where're you going? The second act's about to start!"

"Gonna use the restroom. Back in a flash." He spun and jogged up the stairs.

Why didn't he pee during the intermission if he had to go so bad?

Slade and Colt, sitting directly behind us, didn't glance up at Lachlan as he left. They kept their eyes on the darkened stage. I had no idea Colt and Slade liked shows like this, but when Lachlan told them we were flying to Vegas, they said they wanted to come too.

The musical spectacle that is Cirque du Soleil resumed in dramatic fashion. Lachlan thought I'd like to see their ice show, a high-flying interpretation of Swan Lake. Brightly colored acrobats, skaters, and contortionists made the death-defying moves seem effortless. I could only hope to be that skilled on the silks someday. I had no chance of ever being able to ice skate like the athletes out there jumping ramps and flipping. Amazing.

If Lachlan didn't get back soon, he'd miss the finale.

The scene switched to an all-white stage. A huge iceberg rose up from the ground. Skaters wearing elaborate iridescent costumes swirled and spiraled on the ice. The prince was about to deny his family and claim the beautiful swan as his wife.

The music slowed. All the performers froze like ice sculptures. A hushed murmur rumbled over the crowd.

And Lachlan walked out from behind the stage.

I choked and coughed.

His boots slipped on the ice, and he held his arms out to balance himself. He looked so... human among the icy-white statue people. He was dressed in dark jeans and a black T-shirt, like a man from the wrong universe who had wandered onto the stage.

A vivid blue spotlight shone down on him, reflecting off the ice and highlighting the angles and planes of his face. A performer handed him a microphone.

"Hi, I'm Lachlan."

The crowd cheered for him, and he looked down at the ice with a shy smile. I didn't cheer. I was too busy picking my jaw up off the floor. Why the hell was my man on the stage?

"This show is perfect. These artists never fail during a performance. But what you don't see is the millions of hours of rehearsal to present this superb show to you. I haven't rehearsed anything, and I'm certainly not the best at anything. But I've found a perfect love."

Oh my word. He is not.

"And tonight, in all my humanness, amidst all this unattainable perfection, I ask her to be my wife."

The crowd collectively sighed, heads bobbing around trying to figure out who was the poor victim of his intentions.

He lowered one knee to the ice and held up a ring. He squinted into the light.

"Nevada Lacy, I can't climb silk. I'm unbearingly overprotective. I'll make a lot of mistakes. I'm probably messing this up right now, but I promise you one thing. Our love is flawless. It's beyond this world, and I believe in it more than anything else. I know our love is so strong we can survive even our own humanness. So come down here and say you'll marry me."

Not sure how I managed to move, my legs forced me to stand. All eyes landed on me.

"C'mon now. Don't leave me hanging on the ice down here."

Loud sweeping music ushered me from my seat. When I reached the center aisle, the music peaked. The excitement from the crowd propelled me forward. I had to run to him. I had to get to him as fast as possible. I hit the wall of the stage hard, knocking the wind out of my lungs. He smiled and helped me awkwardly climb up. I jumped in his arms and he fell back, laughing.

We kissed on the ice floor of the stage of Cirque du Soleil.

He held the microphone to my lips. "Is that a yes?"

"Yes, of course."

The crowd went ballistic. He lowered the microphone and kissed me. "I love you."

"You're crazy."

"I am, but I love you."

"I love you too, Lachlan. Forever."

Chapter 11

Six months later

Lachlan

In a VIP booth at Siege, Nev smiled her sweet smile at me as she chatted wedding plans with Crystal. Surrounded by family and friends on her birthday, she looked more gorgeous than ever. She'd gained back her weight, more curves for me to hold on to and a plush ass to spank. Her hair returned to the rusty sunset colors that flowed down her back like lava. Made me feel good, I was giving her what she needed and making her happy. I let her know this by sending her a smile back saying I couldn't wait to get her naked again soon. Her cheeks turned the color of her hair, and she looked away.

Opposite Nev, Tavian sat grinning in the middle of a group of girls from her gym. He'd taken to watching their aerial performances and had become a big fan, of all of them.

Colt, drinking a beer with me and Slade, was telling us a story about a call he responded to today. "So we find pants for the guy, get him dressed, and he takes them off again saying he don't need no goddamn pants to mow his lawn."

Slade slapped Colt's shoulder and pulled a punch to his gut. "Hey, man. I always mow the lawn buck nekkid."

Colt didn't tense at the fake punch. He stayed relaxed, clearly comfortable with Slade. Well, shit. Had Colt swapped Slade into my role as best friend?

No. What we had ran deep. Slade wasn't a threat. Glad to see Colt smiling lately after the darkness in his eyes while Nevada went missing.

The camouflaged net opened, and Rogan lifted his chin at me.

I left the guys and walked up to Rogan. I'd asked him to meet me here so I could give him some intel on the Barebones case. "How's Tessa?"

"She's good. You got something I need to know?"

Rogan tolerated me because I helped Tessa win her case, but he'd never forgive me for dating her to investigate his boss.

"Zook Guthrie's getting out of FCI Englewood in Colorado next week."

His eyes narrowed. "Early release?"

"A few months."

He chewed his lip as his gaze travelled around the guests at Nev's party, but he didn't focus on anyone. I could guarantee his thoughts were one-hundred percent on Tessa and her safety. "He'd better not show up here, or I'll have to kill him."

Yep. Just what I thought. I'd had something on my mind the last couple years I'd never shared with Rogan, but with Zook getting out, I figured he needed all the information. Might keep him from committing murder. "I'd hold your fire till you get the whole story."

"What do you mean?"

"My gut's telling me he didn't do it."

He scratched his head above his ear. "Gonna take a lot more than a gut feeling to convince me."

"He testified at Jeb's trial that he read all the information on the computers he recovered."

Light flickered in Rogan's eyes. "But he can't read."

"Exactly." Zook hid it well, but he'd never learned to read or write.

Rogan glanced outside the booth and smiled as Tessa came up the steps, walking toward us. "That doesn't mean he lied about Lyric."

"No, but it plants a seed of doubt."

Rogan rolled his eyes, hating the *planting a seed* reference from the trial. "I'm not a fan of his, but I'll take what you have to say into consideration."

Tessa came to his side. He wrapped an arm around her and pulled her close. "Hi, Lachlan. I heard it's your girlfriend's birthday."

"She's about to be my wife. Wanna meet her?"

I gave Rogan a head tilt, and he let Tessa go so she could meet my future wife.

Chapter 12

‐‐‐‐‐‐‐

Nevada

Lachlan, Slade, and I pushed through the wooded encampment known as "Tent City" near downtown Brockton. Shanti led the way through the brush like he sensed our purpose and wanted to help. We passed a few empty tents, one locked with a padlock. Lachlan held some branches aside for me as we came to a compact open area. Outside the tent, around a small fire, was a lighter, a spoon, and a loaded syringe.

Slade moved to the tent and slipped up the zipper. Shanti whimpered a little, sensing danger. Slowly, Jeremy came out. He looked young, so young, and again I was struck by how much he looked like Lachlan. Tall, thin, curly brown hair, dark-blue eyes that had seen too much misery.

My dad's spirit came to me and became part of me. When he saw Lachlan at fifteen, trying to buy cocaine, he saw the injustice of a child failed by his parents. A victim of a society where a young man felt desperate enough to hide in a tent and shoot up heroin that could very likely kill him and would surely screw his brain up beyond repair.

Jeremy had the hood of his jacket tightened around his face. "Uh, Johnny, that money I owe you." His feet shuffled in the dirt. "I'm gonna have it soon. I got a job lined up. Just waiting for my first paycheck." His eyes were dead. No light like a teenager should have. Addiction had stolen his light.

I looked at Lachlan and saw all the same emotions on his face. Jeremy represented the horrible path his life could've taken if my dad didn't step in.

"I'm not here for money, Jeremy," Slade said softly. "We're here to talk to you. This is my friend Nevada."

He looked up at me. "I remember her."

"This is Lachlan, her husband. They asked me to take them out here to find you."

"You did?" He looked shocked that anyone would care about him. And that broke my heart. Everyone needed someone to care about them.

Lachlan stepped closer to him, the importance of the step resonating through his whole body. His hunched shoulders heading toward the younger version of himself with purpose. "We want to help you get off heroin, Jeremy. Get on with a good life."

"Are you cops?"

Lachlan held up his hands, palms flat, to show we posed no threat. "I'm FBI and Nevada is DEA."

He looked around, ready to run. Shanti stood up and barked, causing Jeremy to flinch.

"We're not here to arrest you." I stepped next to Lachlan. "We want to help you. Come with us, and we'll get you through detox. You can start again, Jeremy. It doesn't have to be like this, chasing the next high, spending all your money on drugs. Lachlan was a lot like you and look at him now. He has a good life, a loving wife, a good job. He made mistakes too when he was young, but he turned it around. You can do that. You could have that."

"I'm on a waiting list with the city to get into county rehab."

Lachlan put a hand on his shoulder. "No county rehab. Pack your stuff. Come with us right now."

"Crashing is hell, man. I don't know if I can do it."

I placed my hand on his other shoulder and offered him a gentle smile. "You can and you will. We'll be there and help you. But you gotta commit right now. No BS. We help you detox, and you promise to get back in school and get a job."

"Why would you do this for me?"

"Because we're human." Lachlan's voice cut out. "We all fail. But we get back up and try again. We believe you can do it, and we want to be there to see it. Are you in?"

His chapped lips spread into a hopeful smile. "I'm in."

Become a VIP reader

———

Sign up to Bex Dane's VIP reader team and receive exclusive bonus content including;

- The first chapter of Zook (Men of Siege Book Two)

- Behind-the-scenes secrets no one else knows

- Deleted scenes

- Advanced Reader Copies and first look at cover reveals

Get bonus content[1]

———

1. https://www.subscribepage.com/bexzookbonus